ASSASSINATION . . .

Chief Hissler sat in front of the blank screen and drummed his fingers lightly on the desktop. Then, consulting the computer terminal, he punched some numbers and waited. "Let me speak to Captain Wok," he said when the screen came to life. The agent on the other end complied at once.

"Chief Hissler." The captain on the starship looked somewhat disconcerted by this unusual contact from the chief.

"Captain, I've got a new assignment for you. You are to change courses immediately and head for the V-Two sector. You will pick up Captain Deadalus at the spaceport. You will then proceed into free space. Once there you will terminate Captain Deadalus. Before you kill him, you are to try to get some information from him. Use every available means to get him to talk, Captain Wok. The information may be extremely important to the welfare of the Empirical government."

Hissler waited a moment to make sure that there was no misunderstanding. "Deadalus may be on his guard, Captain. You are to proceed with utmost caution. I feel I must advise you, for your own well-being as well as for the success of this mission. Don't try to take him on by yourself. Use every bit of force that's available to you. Deadalus is deadly. He may be the single most dangerous man loose in the galaxy."

STARSHIP ORPHEUS #1

SYMON JADE

PINNACLE BOOKS   **NEW YORK**

STARSHIP ORPHEUS #1: RETURN FROM THE DEAD

Copyright © 1982 by Michael Eckstrom

An original Pinnacle Books edition, published for the first time anywhere.

First printing, March 1982

ISBN: 0-523-41646-6

Cover illustration by Earl Norem

Printed in the United States of America

PINNACLE BOOKS, INC.
1430 Broadway
New York, New York 10018

RETURN
FROM THE
DEAD

ONE

He smiled at the surveillance camera.

The door slid open with an angry hiss.

He turned and winked back over his shoulder at the secretary, who immediately looked away with a flustered blush. Then Captain Deadalus stepped into the office of the chief of the Empirical Secret Police.

The door snarled shut behind him.

Captain Deadalus's medium height and slim build gave no indication that he was one of the secret police's most efficient and deadliest agents. As he approached the huge desk at the far end of the room, the corners of his mouth turned up and his light blue eyes glinted, giving only a hint of the intensity of emotions that lay coiled inside him like a snake.

The silence as he crossed the room was more than casual. Deadalus sat down in the hard, uncomfortable chair facing the desk, meeting the glare of the man opposite with a smile. The silence continued.

On the far side of the desk Chief Hissler

hunched. His nose was like a craggy cliff long exposed to the weather. Sharp and pitted, it jutted out from between his small, black eyes and hooked down toward his thin, bloodless lips.

"You want to tell me just where the hell you've been?" Hissler demanded, breaking the drawn silence.

"The cruiser I was on had some mechanical problems."

Hissler snorted in disgust.

"You should have been back ten days ago, Captain. You were probably screwing around with one of your damn females. Ought to have you demerited."

Deadalus started to reply, but stopped himself.

"What did the board say about my assignment?" he asked after a minute.

"You'd better get it through your head that I don't give a piss what the damn board thinks. You answer to me and if I don't like the way you work, I'll break you down to rank, and there ain't nothing your damn little board of supervisors is going to do about it."

"I was told they were quite pleased."

"Well, I wasn't pleased. You've been getting too fancy. I sent you out on a straightforward assignment and instead you go sneaking around in some assbackwards way . . ."

"But it worked! All I did was . . ."

"I know what you did, damnit, I read your report! And I'm telling you not to do it again. You do only what you're assigned to do. Stop all this fancy business."

2

"I thought that the agent was supposed to use his own judgment in the method of completing the assignment."

"But you aren't supposed to change the damn assignment!"

"I don't! I just interpret the intention . . ."

"Well, don't!"

"Don't what?"

"Don't interpret nothing. Just do what you're told. Nothing more and nothing less. I've had it with you. Step out of line just once more and I swear I'll have you shoveling shit for the rest of your career. And if you think that just because you happen to be my nephew I won't . . ."

"Hardly."

"What was that, Captain?"

Deadalus stifled his reply. They had this same argument every time. He was well aware that his uncle would leap at any opportunity to kick him off the force. That was one of the things that continually prodded Deadalus into being one of the best agents in the secret police. The chief complained about his method only because there was nothing else he could find to fault Deadalus for. Deadalus's record was perfect. He had never been caught and never failed to complete his mission successfully.

Deadalus glanced around the office as Chief Hissler angrily shuffled through some folders.

The office hadn't changed since the very first time he had been in it, seven years earlier. The room was conspicuous for its bare, almost frugal appearance. There was no furniture other than the chief's desk and the chair where

3

Deadalus was sitting. The walls were metallic white, unadorned by any sort of frills. To the unobservant viewer there was nothing to indicate that this office belonged to one of the most powerful men in the entire galaxy.

But Deadalus was far from unobservant and he was aware that the plain white walls were impervious to nearly every type of weapon, from projectiles and explosives to chemicals and radiation. Within the walls was an electronic-static field that made the office immune to outside surveillance. Deadalus was also aware of the arsenal of control buttons imbedded unobtrusively on the desk top. He could only guess at what most of the buttons did, but he knew that if he were to make any violent move toward Hissler, the chief could kill him with the touch of a button.

"This next assignment should be clear enough, even for you," the chief said, breaking into Deadalus's thoughts.

"Assignment! I just got back! What about my recreational leave?"

"You spent your recreational leave in the ten extra days it took you getting back, Captain."

Deadalus groaned, but took the folder that the chief held out to him.

"It's on a planet called Eurydice, out in the V-Two sector. There's a group of artists practicing illegally. The leader, a singer named Flo, used to have a license but it was revoked for breaking her non-political clause. She's attracted a group of kids around her and is causing quite a stir."

4

Deadalus was glancing through the folder as he listened to the chief.

"So why don't the local authorities take care of it? Haven't they been notified?"

"Yes. But the governor has been rather uncooperative."

"So how come you don't change his mind for him?"

"That's precisely what we're doing."

"How? By grabbing this Flo and throwing her in jail?"

"By eliminating her."

Deadalus glanced up sharply.

"You want to kill her just to prove a point to some governor? Seems rather extreme to me."

"You weren't asked for your opinion, Captain. These things have been decided by people who have a great deal more knowledge than you do. You just worry about completing your mission as assigned. As a matter of fact, you're to eliminate two people. There's a young man who helps lead the group."

A grimace passed over Deadalus's face. He perceived from the chief's tone that this mission had more to do with politics than with criminal activity. Deadalus's job was supposed to be to enforce the law, not further someone's political career.

"You must be kidding," Deadalus burst out. "Do you really mean to send me a quarter of the way around the galaxy to kill two innocent people just to prove to some pigheaded governor that he'd better mind his manners?"

"Calm down, Deadalus. First off, they aren't

innocent; they're practicing art without a license."

"That's hardly a capital offense!"

"Secondly, the entire situation has political nuances that you have no knowledge of."

"But why don't you just go after the governor directly if he's the one that's causing the problem?"

The chief lumbered to his feet, his face contorted with rage.

"I am not in the habit of justifying my orders, Captain! And if you want to remain a captain, you damn well better just get your ass out of here and do what you're told! And you'd better not get fancy on this one, or I promise you I'll bust you down to rank faster than you can . . ."

The door rasped shut behind Deadalus, cutting off the sound of the chief's tirade. With the folder under his arm, Deadalus winked at the surprised secretary, who once again blushed at the captain's attention.

"Is something wrong, Captain?" she managed to ask.

"Nothing to worry about. The old man's just got a bad case of indigestion." Deadalus walked quickly toward the exit. "Guess he's been eating too much crow."

Captain Deadalus surveyed the deluxe gaming room on board the large public cruiser. He could have gotten a ride in one of the agency's starships; it would have been a lot faster. But Deadalus had decided that if he had to go out again he was at least going to do it in style.

Deadalus wandered down among the gaming tables. His senses, which were trained to the highest degree possible, automatically took in every minute detail.

Deadalus debated whether he should have dinner first or just start in gambling. He opted for dinner and had just turned to leave when his eye caught a sight in the entryway that made him stop.

She was young, certainly no more than nineteen, and her body was built like it was designed by a master computer. It wasn't her beauty so much as the expression on her face that caught Deadalus's attention. Her fine eyes and mouth were bent in cold rage. If the emotion didn't add any beauty to her features, it at least made them all the more striking.

He watched as she hesitated in the entryway looking around expectantly. Her eyes fixed on someone, and Deadalus looked to see a leering man approach her. By the look on her face, this was the person she was expecting, and yet the man was obviously not in her class. The man had a bulldog nose and heavy jowls which made him look like a common thug.

The man walked directly up to the girl who stood stiffly awaiting his approach. His face was spread in a crude sneer as he took hold of the young lady's elbow and whispered something to her. Deadalus saw the rage on her face momentarily replaced by disgust.

Deadalus decided that dinner wouldn't be any fun by himself. What he needed was the company of a pretty young lady. Walking nonchalantly toward the couple still standing in the entryway, he appraised the man, noting the thickly-muscled neck as well as the heavy-footed way he was standing. Deadalus tensed his wrist, checking his knife sheath, though he didn't think he would have to use it.

Deadalus smiled at the young lady, seemingly ignoring the man altogether.

"Excuse me, miss, but I was just on my way to get some dinner and I was wondering if you would care to join me?"

The young lady's fine eyebrows arched, more in amusement than in surprise.

The thug who still had hold of her elbow, growled deep in his throat.

8

"Clear out, bud."

Deadalus glanced at the man, then looked back at the young lady.

"I'm sorry," he said lightly. "I didn't realize that this charming gentleman was with you."

"Hey! I ought to take your head off!" The man let go of the girl's arm and reached out to push Deadalus.

In a motion so smooth and quick it was probably unseen by anyone else in the room, Deadalus took hold of the man's wrist, yanked down, and twisted. It could almost have been mistaken for a handshake, except for the snapping sound and the strange angle of the man's arm when Deadalus let go.

The smile on Deadalus's face hadn't faltered as he dislocated the man's shoulder. Very painful, but no permanent damage.

From the corner of his eye Deadalus saw the two security guards closing in. Still, he didn't take his attention off the thug's thick face, now covered with pain and disbelief.

The thug gave a low curse and then fumbled at his pocket with his other hand, trying to get out some weapon. Deadalus balanced on the balls of his feet, his eyes taking note of the spot on the man's thick neck where he would bury his knife.

But before the man could get his fumbling hand out of his pocket, the two uniformed guards were there.

"Alright. Let's break it up." The guards stepped between Deadalus and the thug. "Why

9

don't you go cool down." They started moving the other man away.

"You're going to regret this, mister! You don't know who you're fooling with. You're not going to be able to hide. I'll find you and I'll make you wish you were never born."

The thug was led away, holding his injured arm.

Deadalus smiled grimly to himself. The man didn't know it, but those guards had just saved him from certain death.

He saw the girl watching him and he smiled at her.

"He's a bad man to have as an enemy," the girl said seriously.

"Oh? Who is he?"

"Lieutenant Kreps. He's one of Governor Washba's bulldogs."

"I take it then that the lieutenant is capable of carrying out his threats?"

"Quite."

"I see. And what was it that the lieutenant wanted with you?"

The young lady looked him directly in the eye and, half angry and half amused, she said, "I suppose the same thing you want."

Then, without waiting for the surprised Deadalus to reply, she turned toward the exit.

"Shall we go to dinner?"

THREE

The more Deadalus thought about it, the more
he felt he'd been sent after the wrong people. It
sounded as though this Washba character was
the one who needed cooling off. Of course, as
the chief had said, that's what the mission was
really for, indirectly. Killing off this group of
illegal artists was supposed to strike fear and
trembling into the governor. Personally, Deadalus doubted that the man would give a damn.
But the chief never took foolish or unnecessary
action. There must be some connection that
Deadalus hadn't been informed of, and Deadalus didn't like that. There was too much going
on that he was unaware of. He considered anything he didn't know as a potential weapon that
could be used against him.

Deadalus decided to make use of the ship's
library to see what background information he
could acquire.

The library, which boasted a collection of
over a million volumes, was contained in a small
wall of drawers. Everything was recorded on

minute audio-visual microspots. Deadalus selected a general history of the V-Two sector and took it over to one of the private readers. The reader consisted of a thin display screen about the size of a dinner plate and an earphone. The text was contained in the audio, the visual was just supplementary.

The history of the V-Two sector was similar to many of the colonies. Like all habital systems, it was located in the thin band, twenty-five light-years wide, that ran around the circumference of the galaxy about two-thirds of the way from the center. The star, called Gabriel by the colonists, was a G4V spectral-class star and was one of the early sectors investigated. There were three habitable satellites in the Gabriel system. The prime, now named Therminous, was a planet about two point five AU's from the star. The secondary planet, Eurydice, was farther out, about three AU's. Kraton, the third habitable body, was a satellite of a large Jovian planet, seven AU's from the central star. Kraton wasn't very hospitable and had never been fully developed, being almost exclusively a base camp for mining operations.

Therminous was completely self-sufficient by the Fourth World War and survived the ensuing dark ages quite well. The planet had an abundant supply of metal and, until the war, it had an economy based largely on miners and merchants. When Earth succumbed to the chaos of war and the consequent feudal period, Therminous started selling ore to other nearby systems. As time progressed and contact with these systems dwindled, the merchants on Therminous decided to create their own demand and developed the technology to colonize the nearby planet Eurydice. Eventually, even with the new world to develop, the demand for metal ore completely stopped and Therminous, like practically all the other colonies, became exclusively agrarian.

Because it had continued contact with other colonies long after it had lost contact with Earth, and, because of the impetus of developing its own colony, the culture on Therminous thrived through the long period when Earth was wrapped up in feudal chaos and all the colonies became isolated. Its technology declined, of course, as did all the world's, but it wasn't lost completely. And it made a purpose of maintaining knowledge of the past, which, later historians have pointed out, was the main difference between those cultures that progressed and those which declined. Every colony that lost contact with history eventually fell into a decline.

Therminous was unique in another manner. When Earth began its re-conquest of the galaxy, Therminous was one of its early priorities because of the colony's large supply of the heavy metals, which the young Empire desperately needed for its war effort. When Earth first attacked the Therminous forces, the colony did a very peculiar thing. Though fairly well equipped to defend itself, the colony chose not to fight. Instead, its leaders, seeing this as an opportunity to regenerate its long dormant mining operations, drew up a contract to supply all the ore needed for certain concessions on Earth's part. The young Empire, still wobbly on its space-legs, was overjoyed to get the ore without having to fight for it and so quickly agreed to the contract. Consequently Therminous became the only colony that wasn't conquered by the Empire.

Most of the concessions that the Empire had made in the contract were ignored later since Therminous had no way of enforcing them on the growing Empire. But one agreement that the Empire was still trying to find a way to get out of, was that Therminous was to have complete control over the mining and shipping of the ore. The Empire was still trying to find a way to break the colony's control over the ore, and no doubt eventually would, but meanwhile, Therminous was becoming one of the richest planets in the galaxy.

Like all the colonies that survived the age of isolation, Therminous had developed its own religion. And, as everywhere else, the Empire was very careful to incorporate into this religion. The Empire promised not to interfere with local beliefs and customs as long as the Church of Earth was recognized as the highest and supreme authority. Since the alternative was to be persecuted and completely annihiliated, the religious leaders on Therminous did what all the religious leaders on all the other planets did. They agreed.

The Empire used this religious authority with extreme delicacy, making certain that the local

14

leaders at no time felt manipulated. This use of religion was one of the main reasons Earth was able to conquer and keep control over the galaxy.

The general history gave Deadalus a good idea why the chief, or whoever was behind the chief, was unwilling to attack Governor Washba directly. The governor probably controlled all the mining and shipping on the planet and could, if pushed, probably put a halt to all operations. The Empire would, of course, in such a situation take over the mining and shipping. But it would take awhile before they would make it operational again. The ore was so crucial that it would cause serious problems to have any lapse in the supply.

But Deadalus still did not see the connection between the illegal artists and the governor.

Deadalus took out the history and put in a scientific survey of the Gabriel system. He flipped through most of it until he came to the description of Eurydice.

Eurydice was small for a habitable planet, being only one-third the size of Earth. But because of the planet's extremely high concentration of heavy elements, its mass was only one-fifth less than Earth's.

Its mean temperature was rather high, about 102 degrees Farenheit. The climate was fairly well controlled by a large ring of freestanding water built around the one city. This huge moat, as well as use of underground structures and large shrubs, helped keep the outside temperature in the city at least bearable. The build-

15

ings were of course all geothermically controlled.

On the outside of this moat was a ring of farmland which was able to produce the basic food necessities.

The rest of the planet was given to mining, which was done with an economic precision that approached perfection. The wealth from this mining was used to import all the luxuries which were not available on the planet itself.

There was one footnote that caught Deadalus's eye. It mentioned something about an animal known locally as a gato. He looked gato up in the index.

When man first started exploring the stars he had been disappointed to find that there was absolutely no life anywhere in the galaxy except on Earth. But as the certainty of this sunk home, man quickly realized that it was a benefit. Nowhere in the galaxy was there anything for men to fear, neither large intelligent life, nor small bacteria or germs. It was with this knowledge that the idea of colonization really started.

Until then everyone had assumed that to live on another planet would be a constant battle against the environment because of the atmosphere and the landscape. But when people realized that there were no life forms to worry about, they began to think differently. Why not just change another planet to make it habitable? Any planet that was large enough and had the right temperature could be given a suitable atmosphere. And, if enough vegetation was introduced, and some large bodies of water, there would be very little necessary maintenance. With careful use of cloud cover and upper-level ionization, any planet could be heated or cooled to a degree. With the proper use of technology, this process of climatization only took about a century.

The second part of climatization involved the introduction of animal life. Often, the colonists, using genetic engineering, would breed certain characteristics into an animal which would make it more suitable for the particular environment, or would give an animal certain qualities which would make it better equipped for some job. Often they would do such radical genetic changes that they would create a new subspecies.

Because of the method of mining employed when Therminous was colonized they decided that they needed a small, trainable animal to aid in the mining. The animal they chose was the common household cat.

The first change they made was to increase its intelligence to make it more trainable. Then they widened and flattened its front paws, making them flexible enough to grasp objects. Finally they improved its eyesight, making it able to see a greater length of the spectrum.

Many of these animals, which were now called gatos, were at one time in use in the mining operations. And, as it always seemed to happen with genetically-engineered animals, many of them escaped into the wilds where they thrived and continued breeding.

17

The footnote that Deadalus had come across mentioned one thing that these animals learned in the wilds of Eurydice which man hadn't taught them. They had learned how to hunt in packs.

Deadalus put away the science survey with mild frustration. He had learned very little that he hadn't already known, and nothing which could help him unravel all the hidden meanings in this mission. He would just have to wait until he got to Eurydice to see what was going on. And until he filled in a few gaps in his knowledge, he decided to move with extreme caution.

Deadalus stood naked in the middle of the small hotel room. And still the sweat poured down his face. So much for geothermal temperature control.

Actually, it wasn't the temperature that was so awful, or so the tourist desk clerk assured him, it was the humidity. Whichever it was, it was uncomfortable.

Moving as little as possible, Deadalus laid out his arsenal of weapons on the small bed, checking over each one as he removed them from their various hiding places. He had gone to great lengths to hide them while coming through customs. Deadalus was quite adept at smuggling weapons and had never been caught. He had thought that he might run into trouble this time. He had expected Lieutenant Kreps to be waiting for him, ready to carry out the threats he had made earlier on the ship. But Kreps was not to be seen and Deadalus had no difficulty whatsoever getting through customs.

Deadalus had not seen the good lieutenant

since the incident on the ship, but then, Deadalus had hardly left his cabin the entire week of the trip.

The young lady he had rescued from the lieutenant insisted on staying in Deadalus's cabin, claiming she was too frightened of the governor's minion to risk sleeping alone. Deadalus didn't argue.

It turned out that the young lady's meeting with Kreps had not been accidental. Her fiancé was in a detention camp on Eurydice, where he had been sent for political activism. The detention camp was known to be little more than an elaborate torture chamber from which few returned alive. The young lady had been considering trying to buy her fiancé some privileges by doing a few favors for the lieutenant, but at Deadalus's intervention she had changed her mind. She felt guilty about having done so. Deadalus spent the remainder of the trip consoling her.

After checking over the condition of each piece in his arsenal, Deadalus started selecting which ones he would take for the night's activities. With any luck he would be able to wrap up the whole mission tonight and return home in the morning. But there were a lot of things he was going to have to find out first. He wasn't going to do anything unless he knew more about what was going on.

He chose a wrist knife, one of his favorite weapons. Used properly, the knife was quick and absolutely silent. It could be used in a crowded room without anyone even noticing;

but it did have its limitations, especially against a group of people who were armed with more sophisticated weapons.

Deadalus next selected a small, thin, projectile gun, which shot tiny bullets at very low velocity. The bullets carried an extremely powerful explosive which detonated on impact. It was not the explosive power which was so deadly as much as the fact that it caused a fire that burned hotter than magnesium. The result being that the victim was not shattered to pieces, but in a blinding flash was burnt down into a pile of ash. The purpose of this weapon was just the opposite of what Deadalus used the knife for. When he would shoot one member of a group with this, it created an enormous distraction, as if someone had swallowed a flare. It simply took the heart out of most opposition.

Next, Deadalus selected from his cache of explosives. He chose two time-controlled bombs. They were about the size and shape of a small coin and extremely easy to activate, though not unintentionally. To activate them you simply held it between the balls of your two thumbs and twisted your hands in opposite directions. They had four time settings, the longest being twenty minutes. They were each powerful enough to decimate a small building.

Deadalus also made a selection of six small impact explosives. Two of them were relatively harmless, and were actually only a smoke and firework display employed for crowd distraction and cover. Two others contained a gas which, when inhaled, caused a state similiar to extreme intoxication, sometimes even unconsciousness. This drug took effect in about ten minutes and lasted for two to three hours. The last two explosives were simply old-fashioned concussion types that were not very powerful and were intended to be thrown by hand.

All six of these explosives were so small that Deadalus could hold them all in the palm of his hand. They were heavy for their size though, and thus easier to throw.

Deadalus looked over his selection carefully, checking each one again. If the mission was as simple as the chief had made it out to be, he wouldn't need anything but the knife and one of the explosives. Deadalus had the suspicion that it wasn't as simple as it had been made to seem, and if he was going to get caught in a firefight with the governor's police force he didn't want to be caught empty-handed.

Checking the time, Deadalus saw that he had an hour before he would leave. He thought of going down and checking out the guest facilities at the hotel, but in the end decided that it was too uncomfortable to move around and so just got a drink and sat down to relax.

Deadalus's method of work was extremely delicate. While many secret police agents used brute force to accomplish their tasks, Deadalus always used precision. And it was Deadalus's silent precision which usually left more fear.

A good case in point was the incident with the governor of one of the far sectors who had become rather reluctant with his taxes. An agent was sent to encourage him, and this agent went in with guns blazing, knocking down walls and then, with a gun held to the governor's head, insisted that he pay his taxes. The taxes were paid, but the next year the governor simply built stronger walls. So Deadalus was sent. Undercover, Deadalus assessed the situation. He discovered that inside the governor's well-guarded palace, the governor had a prized collection of ancient art tapestries. Deadalus got past all the guards and sophisticated alarms without being discovered and stole the tapestries in lieu of the tax payment. But he didn't just leave it there. With extreme stealth he got into the governor's bedchamber while the governor was sleeping and on the pillow next to the governor's head, Deadalus placed his knife and a note suggesting that all future taxes be paid properly. There had been no further problems with that governor.

Deadalus shook himself out of his reverie. It was time to get started. He dressed as coolly as he could without revealing the weapons, and went down into the street.

It wasn't far so Deadalus decided to walk, feeling that it might be useful to get to know the layout of the city.

The humidity had dropped with the coming of evening and it wasn't bad out. Deadalus passed a few other people hurrying by, but most of the residents evidently used the cooled public transportations.

There were a couple of odd things about the city that, though Deadalus had read descriptions of it, still startled him. The sky was a constant aurora borealis, due evidently to some odd reaction between the stars radiation and the water vapor that was released when the planet was climatized. Another odd thing was the surface dirt of the planet, which was greenish due to an extremely high concentration of copper. This dirt gave a greenish tint to the pavement and building sides. If you got dirty on Eurydice, the color was green, not brown. Deadalus wasn't sure if he liked the color, but fortunately the dust was heavy and didn't blow as easily so the city was much cleaner than many cities that he had been to.

Deadalus had seen a lot of strange natural phenomenon though, and wasn't taken aback by the natural elements of Eurydice. What did strike him though were the buildings.

Most of the actual living quarters and businesses were underground, and the part of the structure above ground was more decorative than functional. Since they served no functional purpose, there were no limitations on the design and structure of these buildings. There were all sorts of strange, twisted spires, high ornate towers, and peculiar open-structure buildings. They were made of every imaginable material and were decorated from top to bottom with carvings and designs. Deadalus had to remind himself that the wealth from the mining on Eurydice had created a new, super-rich class, and like all newly rich people anywhere they needed some manner to display their wealth.

24

As he walked, Deadalus automatically memorized the streets and buildings just in case he needed to find his way in the dark or in a hurry.

When Deadalus had first arrived on Eurydice he thought that there might be a problem making contact with the group of artists whom he was supposed to eliminate. Since they were unlicensed, and therefore illegal, he thought that they might meet only in semisecrecy. To his surprise he found that they performed openly and the first tourist agent he had asked told him of a performance this evening.

It made things easier not to have to arouse any suspicion trying to see the artists. On the other hand, it meant that there might be other innocent bystanders at the performance. And Deadalus hated killing innocent bystanders. It was just too sloppy.

When the building where the performance was to be came into view, Deadalus noticed that there seemed to be a crowd gathered in front of it. As he got closer he noticed a great number of police uniforms among the crowd. He slowed down, evaluating the situation.

There was enough of a crowd though that he didn't worry about being singled out by the police. He joined the people moving toward the entryway and went inside.

The building was smaller than it had first appeared from the outside and Deadalus could see that it was crowded. Along three walls were balconies which had a good view of the stage.

The stage was on the third wall. Instead of being against the wall like most stages Deadalus had seen, this one was long and narrow and stuck halfway into the room like a sort of peninsula.

Most of the people were standing on the ground floor around the stage, where there were no seats. Deadalus noticed the plush seats in the balconies were filled with well-dressed couples, while the standing crowd was dressed much more informally. Deadalus found a place among the people around the stage. The balcony seats were probably reserved for the rich and besides, he felt safer down here.

He looked around and noticed that the great majority of people around him were young, in their early twenties or so. The young man and lady immediately next to him were sharing some kind of baked roll and sipping from a jug. The young man saw Deadalus looking at him and offered him the jug.

Deadalus shook his head and smiled.

"Pretty crowded, isn't it?" Deadalus asked the young man conversationally.

The young man nodded gravely, a look of disgust coming to his face.

"Yes. It gets more and more crowded each time Flo performs. All because of them."

The young man indicated the people in the balconies with his head.

"Them? Who exactly are they anyway?"

The young man looked at Deadalus with surprise.

"I'm a visitor," Deadalus explained. "First time here."

The young man nodded. "Those are the rich bastards who have come here to ogle Flo, the leader of the group. They don't care about the political ideas. They find it amusing to be patrons to a group of artists who speak out against them and all their families. They come here because they know there's nothing we can do about it anyway. They're concerned about impressing each other. It's become a fad to come here. It makes me sick."

Deadalus found the vehemence in the young man's voice interesting. Evidently the new rich class had made some enemies along with their money.

Deadalus looked up at the balconies. The people there certainly seemed to fit the young man's description. He noticed one balcony that had nearly a dozen armed policemen standing in it. As he watched, two men entered and sat down in the seats that were being guarded. One man was huge, over six-feet tall and well over two hundred pounds. For all his weight though he carried himself like a general on a battlefield. The second man was a slight young sandy-haired fellow who looked puny next to the larger man. But then, most anyone would look puny next to him. Deadalus turned back to the young couple next to him.

"Who's that fellow?" he asked, indicating the large man.

The young man looked where he was pointing and then spit down on the ground with extreme disgust.

"That's the king bastard of them all," he said, his voice filled with loathing.

The girl he was with shushed him, looking around fearfully.

"That," the young man continued, "is our good and gracious Governor Washba. May he die a thousand and one deaths."

The young lady put her hand on the man's arm, trying to get him to lower his voice.

The governor! Deadalus looked back up at the man in surprise.

"What's the governor doing at an illegal performance?" he asked.

The young man spit on the ground again, but this time when he spoke his voice was lower.

"See that young man with him? That's the governor's nephew. The good governor is trying to get Flo to marry his nephew. Do you know why?"

Deadalus shook his head.

"He wants to get Flo to marry his nephew because the governor is already married. Our great leader would like to entertain his nephew's wife while his nephew is off in distant places. You see, our wonderful governor is very much in love with Flo."

Deadalus looked up at the balcony in fascination. Things were beginning to make sense.

Suddenly one of the armed guards who had been standing behind the governor started forward, his finger pointing directly at Deadalus.

Deadalus looked at the man with surprise.

His eyes met the wrath-filled eyes of Lieutenant Kreps.

Deadalus watched as the lieutenant turned and motioned to one of the other men in uniform, and then the house lights went out and only the stage was lit.

Moving quickly, Deadalus pushed his way through the crowd until he got to the far corner of the stage. Content that there was enough of a crowd between him and the police, he stopped to watch the show. First, he made sure that there was an exit nearby.

The first performance was a young male and female dance duo. They performed an allegorical ballet. The story revolved around a trapped bird trying to get free. The man, thinking that he was doing the bird a favor, keeps her locked up. The bird eventually dies.

From the crowd reaction around him, Deadalus understood that there were political insinuations in this story. It must have just been local politics, because the crowd seemed to love it, laughing at things which Deadalus couldn't fathom the meaning of. He did notice that the people in the balconies were pointedly less enthusiastic about the piece than were those on the ground level.

The next performer was evidently a favorite and got a loud welcome when he came on stage. The performer was a young man who looked and dressed like the young men in the crowd around Deadalus.

The young man, who introduced himself by the name of Whiskey, carried a small stringed instrument which looked to be some kind of harp. He sat down on a high stool in the middle of the stage, strumming the instrument experimentally and looking around at the audience with a small smile. When the uproar that greeted his entrance died down, he began speaking quietly.

"Most of you know the ancient myth that our planet Eurydice was named for, but there are those of you who have perhaps forgotten.

"Eurydice, who was said to be the daughter of a wood nymph and the sun god, was married to Orpheus, the greatest singer and poet of the ancient world. One day she was bitten by a snake in the grass and died.

"Orpheus was inconsolable. Distraught with grief, he finally determined to seek out the underworld and bring Eurydice back to earth.

"Now Orpheus was no Hercules that he was going to fight death with his bare hands. No, Orpheus was a singer and so it was music he had to use to persuade the god of the underworld to relinquish the spirit of his beloved.

"Orpheus sang, and he sang so sweetly that

he charmed the monsters guarding the path to the underworld. He sang so gently that for the first time in eternity the souls of the tormented damned knew a blessed moment's peace. He sang so sadly that the gods of the underworld agreed to let him have his beloved Eurydice back on one condition. Orpheus was to return to the world of light followed by Eurydice, but he was not to turn around and look at her until he had left the underworld. Orpheus did as he was told, but at the last moment, just before he stepped back into the world of light, Orpheus was assailed by doubt. And doubting, he turned and glanced back at Eurydice.

"That was the last that he ever saw of his beloved."

The young poet paused for a moment, strumming on his instrument.

"The moral of this story is obvious. Our own doubts are as dangerous to Eurydice as are snakes in the grass."

He looked up at the balcony where the governor and his nephew were sitting.

"I would like to dedicate my humble poem to all the glorious patrons of our theater," he said with a mocking smile.

Deadalus could feel a sudden tension throughout the crowd. From the way that the young man on the stage held himself, Deadalus perceived that he had just offered some sort of challenge and was waiting for a reply. When there was none, he turned back to his instrument somewhat disappointedly and began strumming a simple yet strong rhythm. Then he began reciting.

The poem that Whiskey recited was a thinly disguised tirade against government, and against the governor and his nephew in particular. The pretense at generality was so small that Deadalus was able to follow the poem even with the little he knew about the local political situation.

The crowd seemed to have an even clearer idea of what the poet was saying. But this time there was no laughter or loud guffaws. There was dead silence. As if the crowd was waiting with baited breath, Deadalus could feel an electric tension run through the people. Evidently such straightforward criticism of the government was a very daring thing to do. And from what Deadalus had heard about Governor Washba, he could appreciate the daring of the young poet. From Deadalus's view as a secret police agent, the young poet seemed more foolhardy than courageous.

The crowd certainly expected something to happen. Throughout the poem there was not a sound. No one talked, not even a whisper, and there was not even the usual shuffling of feet. It was as if everyone was stunned and motionless with surprise. Or fear. Remembering the riot gun that he had seen the police carrying, Deadalus edged silently toward the nearest exit.

Deadalus found it difficult to understand what this poet Whiskey hoped to gain by his actions. To rebel against an oppressive leader was one thing, but a person should use some common sense. But then maybe the poet knew something that Deadalus did not. Maybe the governor's love for Flo was so great it extended as a shield over the other performers. It seemed difficult to believe, but Deadalus had seen men do stranger things.

The young poet had finished reciting. The silence in the theatre was tense and brittle. Deadalus could feel that it was going to shatter into a thousand shards at any moment.

"Cut the bastard's tongue out."

It was definitely not a shout. It was hardly more than a mutter. But it came from the balcony with a heaviness that echoed in every corner of the silent building.

Deadalus paused in his stealthy movements towards the exit and looked back over his shoulder. The comment had not come from the governor's balcony, but from some other section. Before the echoes died, someone from the crowd on the ground shouted back.

"It's a public performance. Anyone who doesn't like it can leave."

The reply seemed to waken the crowd from its silence. There was the whispering and muttering of agreement and the sound of shifting bodies, as if everyone on the ground level was turning from the stage and looking instead at the balconies which surrounded them on the walls.

There was another comment from the balcony and this time a chorus of shouts from the ground floor. Soon everyone was shouting.

Deadalus moved quickly toward the exit, no longer needing to disguise his movement. There was going to be a riot, no way out of it now. Even with the police so heavily armed, the crowd was going to feel pressed to live up to the young poet's daring. Perhaps that had been the poet's whole intent.

The sound of the loud and angry voices was escalating dramatically. Deadalus put his hand in his pocket and gripped his gun. He thought he might end up fighting his way free out of the crowd. At any moment he expected the shouting to be replaced by fighting.

With a jarring suddenness, a hush fell over the crowd. Deadalus looked back over his shoulder in surprise, and then he completely forgot about any desire to leave.

The young poet had left the stage and standing in a single white spotlight, was the most striking woman Deadalus had ever seen.

She wore a loose flowing gown that gave off shimmering hints of rainbows as if it were made out of the sky of Eurydice. Like the sky, it was transparent. As she turned in a silent semicircle, looking from one corner of the crowd to the other, Deadalus could see, between the shimmers of rainbows, glimpses of her firm breasts and flat stomach. The glimpses were so fleeting they merely teased the eye and made him wonder if it was an illusion.

The lady had large, dark eyes and long black hair that flowed down over her shoulders and halfway down her back. She stood erect and reminded Deadalus of some angry goddess from ancient mythology. She turned slowly, her dark eyes taking in the audience. Wherever her gaze fell, all sound and movement ceased. When she finished looking from one end to the other, the theater was once again in complete silence.

Softly, so softly, she began to sing.

It was just a simple love song, almost a lullaby, but her soft, high voice was so beautiful that it filled the entire building as if with flowing water.

Deadalus stood transfixed like the rest of the crowd, feeling her song wash over him. When the song was over, there was unanimous applause. The tension that filled the theater to the breaking point only moments before was gone, and there was no longer any division or antagonism in the crowd. They stood as one, sharing in the experience.

Three musicians joined the singer on the stage and she sang another song, this one with a faster, happier rhythm. Deadalus realized why the old vendor outside had called Flo a siren. She could get the crowd to stamp their feet and clap their hands as easily as she had moments before silenced them from their near riot frenzy. She was in complete control of the crowd's emotions, and she could do anything she wanted to with them. While she was singing in front of them, everyone in the crowd was madly in love with her.

It was a combination of physical beauty and her voice, though her singing was the greater attraction. The next song was an old ballad about justice and injustice, change and revolution, and mostly peace. The song complained that things were wrong, but it didn't move the crowd to anger as the young poet had earlier. Instead it filled them with feelings of the nobility of man and the belief that injustice would be overcome, but peacefully.

The ballad was long and slow. Throughout the song the audience stood completely entranced, listening. When the song was over, Deadalus felt as if he had been on a long journey.

The house lights came on and the crowd was stamping and applauding madly, calling for more. Deadalus was clapping as vigorously as everyone else. He couldn't take his eyes off the beautiful lady on the stage solemnly bowing to the crowd's wild adulation.

Even amid the overpowering emotions that filled him, something fought to the surface of his mind. A warning system so ingrained it could never be overcome, even by the panic of emotions, burst into his consciousness like alarm bells.

He caught a movement out of the corner of his eye which was out of sync with the rest of the crowd. Deadalus dropped his hands and whirled in the direction of the motion.

Fifteen feet away a uniformed policeman was taking aim through the crowd. The muzzle of the gun wavered as the policeman was jostled and then it came to rest.

It was pointing directly at Deadalus, of course.

SIX

The muzzle of the policeman's gun sparked with electric static and the spot where Deadalus's head had been was empty.

Deadalus had simply ducked. Not the most sophisticated defense maneuver, but functional. This time it proved sufficient, though just barely in time.

It did have an unfortunate consequence for the young man who had been standing behind Deadalus.

The unintended victim crumbled to the floor next to where Deadalus was crouching. The policeman's gun was perhaps only a stun weapon as Deadalus saw no signs of damage when he glanced at the young man on the floor next to him. He wasn't going to take the time to find out. Besides, for Deadalus to be stunned and captured would be the same as death, if Lieutenant Kreps had any say about it.

Deadalus stood and quickly started pushing his way through the crowd toward the nearby exit. The policeman wouldn't be able to get a good aim on him with all these people about. But Deadalus was going to have to run fast once he got out on the open street.

He hadn't gone two steps before he saw another policeman in front of him pushing toward him. Deadalus turned and saw a third coming from the other side. They had him pinned.

Evidently someone hadn't been as enthralled with the singer's performance as Deadalus had been, and Deadalus thought he knew who.

There were some shouts of alarm as the crowd discovered the fallen man. When the crowd realized that he had been shot by the policeman, there was a general movement away from the victim. Everyone's immediate concern was to demonstrate that they had nothing to do with him.

This movement away from the scene worked to Deadalus's benefit. The pack of people was so thick that it stopped the progress of the three policemen who were closing in on him. Deadalus thought quickly.

He didn't want to use his own gun or any of the explosives he had with him. The crowd was too thick and too many bystanders would be hurt. The crowd worked to his advantage as well. The policemen would be more hesitant to fire their weapons. Not out of concern for bystanders, but because the crowd would probably panic and stampede for the exits, trampling many underfoot, including the policemen. The policemen would have to get very close to Deadalus before they could apprehend him. And Deadalus always had his knife.

The people around Deadalus made a sudden rush toward the exit. Pushed by the mass of people, Deadalus kept his eyes on the policeman between him and the door. The policeman looked as if he would panic under the rush of people trying to get to the exit, but he quickly assessed the situation and allowed himself to be pushed back to the doorway, where he pulled himself to one side, freeing himself from the funnel of people who were trying to get through the door. The policeman braced himself against the wall next to the exit and watched the stream of people passing by. Anyone trying to leave through that door would easily be within his reach.

Deadalus slipped his knife into his hand and allowed the press of the crowd to move him toward the door. The majority of the audience in the theater had taken no notice of what was going on in the small section around Deadalus and they were still loudly applauding the singer. There was a roar of appreciation as something happened on stage, but Deadalus was too busy to turn around to see what had happened.

Ducking and hiding behind people as much as he could, Deadalus worked his way slantwise across the stream of people so that he would be directly next to the waiting policeman. The man had to watch the people passing in front of him and could only afford an occasional glance at the rest of the crowd and so was unable to spot Deadalus. Deadalus glanced over his shoulder and saw that the other two policemen had converged and were pushing through the crowd as fast as they could toward him. They were easy to spot because of their uniforms, but Deadalus reasoned that he blended into the crowd and would be much harder to keep in sight. They wouldn't be able to do anything until they were out in the street.

Deadalus kept his eyes on the policeman by the door as he drew nearer. The policeman didn't see him until he was pressed right next to him.

When the policeman spotted Deadalus, he reached one hand to grab him, while his other hand went for the gun that he had holstered. Deadalus's shock of the policeman's casual motions revealed that he was expecting not to meet with resistance, especially not with anything deadly. Deadalus felt a twinge of guilt as he drove the knife under the man's ribcage, piercing the heart. The policeman was as innocent as anyone else in the crowd. Deadalus could not afford any chance of falling into Lieutenant Kreps's hands. Besides, the policeman was much too careless.

Deadalus instantly withdrew the knife and was on the street before the astonished policeman had slumped to the floor.

Deadalus moved quickly but did not attract undue notice. Most of the people had preceded him out the door and had stopped in the street. They stood about in small groups as if uncertain why they had come out. Some looked back toward the door as if they would have gone back inside if there weren't so many people still streaming out.

Deadalus dodged between these groups of people and around the corner of the building. There he met another group of people coming out a large double door. These people were not rushing; instead they were talking and laughing. Deadalus heard exclamations and praise for the performance which had ended. Farther up the street Deadalus spied the young poet Whiskey, who had come close to causing a riot earlier. The young man had his shoulders hunched as if in dejection and was headed toward a doorway that led underground. Deadalus decided to follow him and hurried down the street.

The doorway led to an underground train. The young poet was walking slowly so Deadalus was able to get close enough not to lose him. Deadalus got on the train behind the young man and took a seat where he could observe him without being obvious. The performer sat with his hands in his pockets and his head bent, staring at the floor. His face nearly danced with changing emotions, going from anger to misery to wry humor to anger. Not once did he glance up and look around and Deadalus had no fear of being noticed by the poet.

Deadalus went over the recent events in his mind. He was going to have to be constantly on guard now against the governor's police. There would be a general alarm out and probably a good description of him. And this time they would all be told that he was armed and dangerous. If he got cornered again he wouldn't get out quite so easy.

Deadalus shrugged off this worry. He had been expecting trouble with the governor's men anyway, and now that the trouble was of his own making, it might lend itself to his advantage. If there was any question about his behavior, no one would likely look for any deeper motive than his argument with the lieutenant. It would therefore be easier to keep his identity as a secret police agent unknown if he was captured. Also, it would make it nearly impossible for them to predict his actions.

Deadalus's main worry now was his mission. He didn't like it. It was stupid, wasteful, unjust, and, worse yet, he probably wouldn't accomplish his objectives. It was clear why his superiors thought that killing Flo and her group of illegal artists would bother the governor. The man must be head-over-heels in love with her. There could be no other reason why he would tolerate the sort of performance that had happened today. But to kill the lady, though it would upset the governor, didn't seem like it would bring him back into line with the Empire, unless there was still more that Deadalus was unaware of.

Still, it didn't seem right to kill the lady when the man they were after was the governor. There should be some better way of doing it. It seemed like the lady would have much more value alive than dead. Deadalus objected to his mission. He was going to have to see if there wasn't some possible variation on his instructions which would be more suitable. This was one mission he wasn't going to rush.

And there was always the possibility that there was something going on that he didn't know about.

Deadalus looked at the young poet he was following, the man who had introduced himself on stage as Whiskey. Deadalus knew that his name was Winchester J. Milton and he was the son of one of the early settlers on Eurydice. His father had been one of the rich mine owners but due to some business intrigue, had become paupered. The young man's father had been so dejected at his change in fortunes that he had killed himself. Whiskey had held down various odd jobs, getting in trouble twice with the authorities because of political views. Then he joined Flo's group and had shown himself to be a fairly versatile poet.

Deadalus knew a lot about the young man who was still looking at the floor in dejection, because Whiskey was the other artist he had been sent to kill.

Whiskey took the train for four stops and then got off suddenly. Deadalus was right behind him. They ended up going only four or five blocks from the theater. Deadalus wasn't sure what the young man was doing. It would have been quicker to walk. But from the way the young poet acted, Deadalus concluded that he had intended going somewhere different when he first got on the train and had changed his mind after he was underway.

The section of town they were in was less ornate than the other areas that Deadalus had seen. The buildings were more functionally designed and the decorations were less elaborate. There were also quite a few more people on the streets, going in and out of the buildings, which Deadalus assumed housed businesses.

Whiskey walked down the main street and then turned up one of the side streets. He no longer looked dejected, only angry. Deadalus followed him and saw him go through a door and down some stairs. Deadalus waited a minute and then followed him in.

Downstairs Deadalus found himself in a crowded room which seemed to be a cross between a bar and a card room. There was no professional gambling, only friendly games between men who had stopped in for a breather before going home from work. Deadalus saw Whiskey sitting alone at a small table on the far side, a half-finished drink in his hand.

Deadalus walked over to the automatic drink vendor, punched out a drink, and then walked around the room, keeping the young man in sight out of the corner of his eye.

He wasn't sure what he wanted with the young man. He had started following him on a whim. He needed more information before he could act. He wasn't going to complete his mission until he had a better idea what was going on. Not thinking of any better way, Deadalus decided that he might as well go over and try to talk to Whiskey. Maybe with a couple drinks and the right listener, the young man would become talkative and reveal something which would help Deadalus decide what to do.

"Excuse me, but isn't your name Whiskey?"

The young man looked up at Deadalus with surprise and suspicion.

"Yes."

"I thought as much. I happened to see your recitation this evening. Quite moving."

The young man stared at him openly and Deadalus could see that there was no sign of backing down in those eyes.

"Look mister, I don't know what you want. I'm just trying to have a peaceful drink. Now if you want to start an argument or something, go ahead and start it."

Deadalus smiled at the young man's hostile challenge.

"I'm sorry if I've offended you or transgressed one of your local customs," Deadalus said carefully. "But you see I'm a stranger to Eurydice, and where I come from bars are meant for friendly conversation."

Whiskey looked down at his glass, somewhat abashed.

"Yeah, well, I'm sorry. Guess I'm just not in a friendly mood."

"Why don't you let me buy you another drink?" Deadalus suggested. "Your glass seems to be empty."

Whiskey looked at him suspiciously, but he wasn't going to turn down a free drink.

Deadalus got him a refill and brought it back and sat down at the table. Whiskey nodded thanks and took a long gulp from the drink.

"You say you're just visiting? What did you think of the performance?" Whiskey asked after he had gulped down half the drink.

"It wasn't exactly what I expected."

"How so?"

"Well, no one told me that I might find myself in the middle of a riot. You really got them started there, didn't you? I thought for sure that the whole place was going to bust loose after your poem and I was going to find myself between two sides of an argument which I knew nothing about."

The young man grinned sourly.

"Yeah, almost had them," he agreed, his voice expressing his obvious disappointment. "That sure would have been something."

Deadalus couldn't understand why the poet wanted to cause a riot.

"It would have been something is right. It would have been a massacre from what I saw of the policemen's weapons."

The sharpness in Deadalus's tone pulled the young man's head up. His eyes studied Deadalus for a minute and then he shrugged.

"They end up killing us one way or the other anyway. It would have been nice to see some of them go down with us for a change."

Deadalus studied the young man with interest. With a little discipline and training, Whiskey would make a good ally. If he kept his present headlong habits, the young man was going to get killed before Deadalus had a chance to get any information out of him. Deadalus got up and got them another drink.

Whiskey took his without question and drank it half down in one gulp.

"I know two of those damn bastards that wouldn't have gotten away. I had my eye on that fat-bellied governor and his squirmy little nephew."

Whiskey's voice had gotten louder from the drink and a couple of heads turned toward them from nearby tables. Deadalus heard muttered threats about what would happen to a loud-mouthed punk if he didn't keep his revolutionary opinions to himself. Two men who aparently worked for the bar came over to the table.

"Look, buddy," the bigger of the two said to Whiskey, "this is a nice peaceful bar and we don't want no trouble. You keep your voice down or we're going to have to throw you out. And we highly recommend that you change your topic of conversation to something a little more congenial, if you get my meaning."

The young man glared at the two men and sipped his drink.

"That poem of yours was really pretty good," Deadalus said, trying to change the subject. "Have you been writing poetry long?"

Whiskey took the bait and began talking about himself and his poetry and how long he had been involved with the group's public performances. Deadalus very delicately led his questions into areas he thought might be helpful. He asked about the activities of the group, how often and where they met, what kind of things they had done, and so on. The young man talked freely and Deadalus kept supplying the drinks, but Whiskey said absolutely nothing which could help him. Everything he said about the group was exactly what Deadalus already knew from the report. The only thing of any significance was that the governor was in love with Flo and allowed them to continue performing even though they weren't licensed and even though some of their political views were not exactly compatible to how he was running the sector. If there was anything else going on, Whiskey evidently didn't know about it. From all indications, if there had been anything else going on, the young poet should have been right at the bottom of it.

Deadalus finally decided that there was no information that Whiskey could give him. The young man was too drunk to be able to deceive someone with Deadalus's training. There was obviously nothing more to know about the group.

Deadalus stood and was just about to offer to help the young man home when he saw Whiskey's bleary eyes suddenly come into sharp focus and his whole body became rigid.

Deadalus followed the direction of the poet's gaze and saw, standing at the foot of the stairs, a long shawl wrapped around her shoulders and looking around as if searching for someone, the beautiful singer whom he had been sent to kill.

Deadalus decided that he would have another drink.

SEVEN

Flo looked around until she spotted Whiskey and then hurried over to the table. She was wearing the dress she had worn during the performance, but the long shawl concealed it. Her long hair had been pulled back and tied, better revealing the sharp features of her cheekbones and forehead. Deadalus could see by her face that she was angry.

Flo stood next to the table, glaring down at Whiskey who hadn't moved since she had come in.

"Well, I hope you're satisfied with yourself," she said angrily. "You almost ruined everything."

Whiskey looked at her for a moment.

"I'm sure you patched it up with your wonderful little governor." The young man's voice was stiff, as if trying to hold something in.

The lady stood straighter than before, and she was silently glaring at the young poet. Deadalus watched her eyes and could see that underneath the anger was worry and concern. He stood up.

"Could I get you a drink?" he asked her, breaking the tense silence.

Flo looked at him seemingly for the first time. She hesitated as if considering leaving.

"I'm sorry. Yes, I guess I would like a drink. I certainly need one."

She sat and Deadalus went and got them all another drink. There was a long awkward silence as both Flo and Whiskey sipped at their drinks, staring at the table.

Deadalus sat back and studied Flo. Her beauty was absolutely extraordinary, but what he found even more alluring were all the strong emotions that played over her features. There was the pride and anger as well as a certain tiredness, as if she had been through some difficult ordeal. There was also a strong concern about Whiskey, and as Deadalus studied her he decided that was the emotion which was strongest at the moment.

"Sometimes, Winchester, I think you like to cause trouble just for trouble's sake."

Her tone was scolding and Deadalus noted the use of Whiskey's proper name. He looked at the young man, knowing what his reaction would be.

Whiskey's head jerked up as if slapped and his eyes blazed at Flo.

"I don't cause the trouble. It's them, your fat-assed governor and his wimpy little dog of a nephew. They're the ones who cause the trouble. That damn tyrant has been causing trouble for years. I'm just trying to bring some of their trouble home to them. I'm just trying to give that bastard back a little of what he's been giving out for years."

"You'll get nothing done your way and please lower your voice." Flo's words were sharp and quiet.

A silence had fallen over the bar as people turned to look at Whiskey. Deadalus pushed his chair back. From his experience with bars, he knew it was about time to leave.

Unfortunately Whiskey didn't quite see it that way.

"No! I will not lower my goddamned voice! I'm tired of whispering my disgust. I'm tired of putting my discontent into pretty rhymes and witty lines. The governor is nothing more than a fat jackal, and I'm tired of smiling and nodding and pretending that he isn't. I'm tired of cringing."

"You don't understand," Flo pleaded. There was some muttering from the other tables.

"The hell I don't. You and your so-called peaceful methods and womanly ways. I'm through curtseying to a man who ought to be strung up by his thumbs, flayed, and fed to the gatos."

Whiskey was no longer looking at Flo but at the rest of the people in the bar. Deadalus groaned. The damn fool kid was looking for a fight. There would be no way that Deadalus would be able to get him out of the bar now.

Deadalus sat back and took a sip of his drink. "The young punk ought to be taught some manners," one of the men said, loud enough for Whiskey to hear.

"Yeah? Well, who's going to do the teaching? In my opinion anyone who lets such a weasel as the governor push them around without complaining ain't man enough to get to his feet and fight."

Deadalus, who had been watching the other patrons, glanced back at Whiskey, noting that the young man evidently knew what he was doing, even drunk. Whiskey was sitting with his feet planted firmly on the floor, his center of balance shifted forward so that he could get quickly to his feet. His right hand was clenched tightly on the back of the empty chair with the evident intention of putting it to some use.

There was a chorus of angry voices in reply to the young man's challenge and Deadalus counted ten men who got to their feet and started over in Whiskey's direction.

Flo put her hand on Whiskey's arm, but he just shrugged it off. Deadalus saw that the young man was smiling now, as he sat for a moment eyeing the men who were grouped together threateningly.

The men were mostly middle-aged, and they looked like they worked at manual labor. They weren't looking for a fight, but they weren't the type to let Whiskey's words go unchallenged.

Still, as they started over, they seemed a bit uncertain, as if hoping that the mere show of force would cause Whiskey to back down and leave the bar of his own accord. The young man evidently saw this hesitancy as well and used it to his advantage. Instead of waiting for them to get better set, Whiskey went into action.

In one quick motion the young man came to his feet, picking up and swinging the chair, smashing it into the nearest man and sending him to the floor with a bloodied head. In one leap he was on the next man with his fists.

Because the men were still bunched together and because the tables were in the way, they were unable to come at Whiskey in force. The young man was making good use of this moment by felling as many of his individual opponents as he could. He knocked the second man out with three well-placed blows and had turned on a third before his surprise attack had even hit home to the rest. Then there was a sudden clamor as tables went flying and everyone began yelling. The brawl broke out in full earnest.

Deadalus sipped at his drink, watching. He was impressed with the way that Whiskey handled himself. The young man had flattened a third before the other seven men could get to him. And even under the weight of such numbers he was still putting up a good fight, though it couldn't last long of course.

Deadalus smiled and took another sip of his drink before he realized that Flo was trying to say something to him.

Her face was extremely pale and her fingers dug into Deadalus's arm. She wasn't screaming or yelling and Deadalus had to lean forward to hear what she was saying.

"Please, please, you must help him. They'll kill him for sure. Please."

Deadalus gritted his teeth. Getting into a barroom brawl was about the stupidest thing he could do right now. There were too many things on the line. Of course, he had enough explosives to bring the whole building down, or he could pull out his gun and start blasting people to pieces, but that didn't seem advisable. What he ought to do is just run for the nearest door like any scared salesman would do.

Instead, he looked into Flo's pleading eyes and smiled.

The men were in a circle around Whiskey and they seemed intent on killing the young man. Deadalus came up behind the closest man, and grabbed him by the neck. Even though the man outweighed Deadalus by a good eighty pounds, he flipped him over his shoulder, throwing him ten feet, where he smashed into the wall and fell, unconscious.

Before the man had hit the wall, Deadalus was on the next man. With two quick blows to the man's unguarded neck, the man fell to his knees, grasping his throat and gasping for air in agony.

By this time the men began to realize that they were being attacked, and a third man turned towards Deadalus, only to be met with a foot in the groin, which lifted him three inches off the floor before he crumbled into a heap.

Four men remained of the original ten, and they forgot about Whiskey and jumped on Deadalus. They were strong and willing, but it would have taken ten times their number to match Deadalus in hand-to-hand combat. And even then they would have found themselves hard pressed without weapons.

Deadalus had to hold back many of his blows. So much of his training was geared towards killing. He was an expert at inflicting a quick fatal blow, but he had no desire or intention of killing any of these men. There was no need to. None of this was their fault. They had just come here for an evening drink and a game of cards with the boys. Then Whiskey had insisted on starting a fight, which none of them really wanted. Now they were facing some man who could turn their insides to pulp before they could even land a punch. It just wasn't fair.

Careful not to inflict any permanent damage, Deadalus put three of the four men out of commission in approximately fifty-seven seconds. The fourth man stood staring at Deadalus in shock, too surprised to run. It was obvious that he wasn't going to come anywhere near Deadalus, and Deadalus left him alone.

After the uproar of the brawl, the bar seemed suddenly quiet. The patrons who had not taken part in the fight were standing to the side, out of the way, their eyes wide and mouths agape. The men were strewn across the floor, unconscious, bleeding, groaning, or gasping. From the center of this melee, Whiskey was struggling, trying to get to his feet.

Deadalus stepped over and helped him up, smiling when he realized that through his broken teeth and bloodied lips, the young man was

57

still muttering challenges, evidently ready and willing to keep fighting.

Deadalus found Flo at his side, helping to hold up the young Whiskey who couldn't manage to stand by himself.

Suddenly, through the silence, there came the pounding of feet on the outside pavement. The door opened and a scared voice yelled down:

"Police!"

EIGHT

Deadalus cursed himself. He knew he shouldn't have gotten involved in the brawl. It was Whiskey's fight; he should have let the young fool get himself killed.

Everyone in the bar was headed toward the exits as the commotion on the street above grew louder. Alone, Deadalus could probably fight his way out, but if he tried to help Flo and Whiskey, who couldn't even stand by himself, he was sure to get apprehended. To fall into the police's hands now was to be worse than dead.

Deadalus came to a quick decision and took Whiskey's arm from around his shoulder and leaned the young man against a table.

He smiled grimly at Flo.

"It was nice meeting you. Perhaps I could see you some other time, under different circumstances. But I've got to go now," he said.

He turned and headed toward the nearest stairway that led to a door on the street.

"No, wait," Flo called after him.

Deadalus spoke over his shoulder.

"Listen, I've helped you all I can. I can't do anything more."

"Yes, I understand. But don't go that way, they're sure to get you."

Deadalus stopped and turned around.

"You know another way out of here?"

"There's a small service tunnel in back. It takes you to where you can catch the underground. There's a lot of people on the trains, the police will never spot you, but you'll have to hurry."

Deadalus hesitated, knowing that he should take her advice and get out of there as quickly as he could.

"Come on," he said, walking over and helping her with Whiskey. "I'll take him, and you lead the way."

"No. You've done enough. I'll take care of him. It's alright."

Deadalus lifted the young man and put him over his shoulder. The young man, though slightly shorter than Deadalus, was stockier and weighed more. He wouldn't be able to carry him far like this, but for a short distance, he could go fairly fast. He would also be able to keep his gun hand free.

"Really, you don't need to do this," Flo said, though she didn't move to stop him.

"I'm not going to let him get beat up by the police after I did all that work to keep him from getting beat up by this crowd. Come on."

He smiled at her and to his surprise Flo blushed and turned away, leading quickly toward the rear of the bar. They went through an area what looked like a storage area. Flo hesitated, looking around. She moved with uncertainty, but after a few steps she saw what she was looking for, and once again moved quickly.

She led the way into a dim and narrow tunnel which ran a short ways and then opened into a larger tunnel. This tunnel had tracks like those Deadalus had seen used by the commuter trains. Along one wall was a narrow walkway. Flo hurried along, Deadalus following warily, the moaning Whiskey still draped across his shoulders. Soon the tunnel curved and Deadalus could see that it led into another tunnel.

Where the two tunnels met, Flo stopped and waited for Deadalus to catch up. The new tunnel was brightly lit and Deadalus could hear the murmuring sound of people. He caught up with Flo and slid Whiskey off his shoulders, leaning the young man against the wall. Deadalus could see that the new tunnel was like the one in which he had caught the underground train while following Whiskey. The waiting platform was noisy and crowded with people.

"Your young friend here is bound to attract a little attention, don't you think?" Deadalus looked at Flo.

"We'll wait here until the next train comes. Once we get inside it'll be all right."

Deadalus nodded, keeping his eyes on the crowd. The lady sure didn't get flustered easily. She acted as though she did this everyday. Maybe she did.

Deadalus tried to think what effect the events of the last few hours had on his mission, but he quickly stopped. He didn't like the possibilities that came to mind.

"Where do you plan to take him?" he asked Flo, whom he realized was watching him with interest.

"My apartment would be easiest. And safest. How about you? Where are you headed?"

Deadalus told her the name of the hotel where he was staying. He tensed at the heavy frown that bent her fine mouth. She looked disturbed and Deadalus had just learned that she didn't get disturbed easily. He wondered if perhaps he had given too much away.

"You're a visitor here?" she asked, her voice mirroring the concern on her face.

"Is that bad?"

She studied him steadily. "It only means that the police will have no trouble finding you. In fact they will probably be waiting for you in your room when you could get there. And I don't think you would very much enjoy visiting with our police on Eurydice. They don't have good manners. Is there anywhere else you could go?"

Deadalus shook his head, too angry with himself to speak. This mission was going from bad to worse and most of it was his fault. He hadn't been thinking clearly. And to have gotten involved in that brawl had been the height of stupidity. If the governor's men caught him now, his cover as a traveling salesman wasn't going to wash well. And they wouldn't hesitate killing him since he had helped an obvious revolutionary. Not that it really mattered that much. He was going to have to stay out of the governor's reach simply because of his run-in with Lieutenant Kreps. Only now he had no back-up defense. If he got caught, he wouldn't be able to talk his way out by claiming empirical immunity.

"Why don't you come to my apartment until we can figure something out? After all your help it would be the least that I could do."

The arrival of the underground train cut off any possibility of answering. They waited until most of the people on the platform had filed in, and then, with Whiskey between them, they hurried forward just barely making it inside before the doors automatically closed.

They attracted a few stares as they sat, but most of the people just look bored, as if they were used to seeing all sorts of things going on.

By the time they arrived at Flo's apartment, Whiskey had regained consciousness.

"Who won?" he asked, even before he had time to groan from pain, as if to find the answer to that question had been his whole reason for coming back to life.

"Take it easy, Whiskey. We're going to take care of you." Flo pointed to a place on the couch where they could lay him down.

"Who won?" he asked again, more insistently.

"The police won this one, buddy," Deadalus replied, laying the injured young man down where Flo had indicated before she left the room to get some bandages and medicine.

"No!" Whiskey seemed very upset. "How

many? How many did I get? I remember one, maybe two. How many?"

"At least three, Whiskey."

"Three? Then I won," he said with a smile which was a rather gruesome spectacle of bloody teeth and swollen lips.

Deadalus realized that the young man had been fighting against overwhelming odds for so long that he really had no concept of what it meant to come out on top. To him success was when he could inflict more damage on a greater number of his opponents before he himself got trampled.

Flo came back with the medicinal supplies and they patched up the young man as best they could. Deadalus checked and made sure that there were no broken bones or other serious damage. Whiskey had actually survived the beating remarkably well. Deadalus was beginning to suspect that the young man had plenty of practice.

As they patched, Whiskey recited snatches of poetry through his puffed lips and seemed to be in good spirits, except that he was frustrated that he couldn't open either eye, both swollen shut.

Flo gave him an injection of pain supressant and put cold compresses on his eyes, and in a few minutes the young man had drifted to sleep.

Flo stood.

"Would you care for a drink? I'm sorry, I don't believe I even know your name."

Her eyes were on him and Deadalus felt a sensation similar to how he had felt during her performance. He had to steady himself before answering.

"My name is Deadalus and yes, I think I could use a drink."

She got them each a drink and they sat down at a small table that was in the corner of the room.

"The young man certainly seems to have a head for finding trouble," Deadalus commented.

"Yes," she hesitated searching for the right words. "He doesn't usually start fights with just anybody, though. I'm afraid that he was rather upset."

"So he told me. Before you came."

"Oh?"

"We were talking about the performance. I was there. It seems he was rather disappointed that he didn't cause a riot."

Flo shook her head and removed her shawl, placing it over the back of the chair.

"He doesn't seem to understand how things work," she said.

Deadalus forced himself to keep his eyes on her face.

"How do things work?" he asked, somewhat stiffly.

Flo studied him carefully.

"I don't suppose it would do any good to ask exactly who you are, would it, Deadalus?"

"I think that the incident in the barroom

would be enough to show my loyalties. I'm running from the same police you are running from."

She smiled. "On Eurydice everyone runs from the police. But I don't mean to sound ungrateful, Deadalus. I really appreciate what you did for Whiskey. I probably appreciate it more than he will." She laughed lightly, easing the tension that had gathered between them.

"I guess my politics aren't a secret anyway," she continued. "If you saw today's performance, or any of my performances, you know how I feel. I feel that a government can only govern with the consent of the people. If the people on Eurydice and other worlds would only wake up and realize how unsuitable the Empire is, then they would shake it off and form their own governments.

"Whiskey is against authority. He thinks that we should be fighting Governor Washba as well as the Empire. He doesn't realize the governor is just a puppet of the Empire, that his only power comes through the authority of the larger government. He doesn't understand that we, that I, can use the governor to our advantage."

Her gaze met his unflinchingly. "You see, the governor thinks he has control over me because he can arrest me any time he likes for practicing art without a license. On the other hand, I think that I am in control. I'm sure you've heard that the governor fancies himself in love with me. Well, a woman knows how to use that to her advantage. Of course, as soon as he's certain

66

that I'm just leading him on, he'll throw me in jail. But we'll see who wins in the end."

"Win!" Deadalus felt a sudden rush of emotions. "You're as bad as Whiskey, thinking he's won because he knocked down three of them before they smashed him. What is it that you think you're going to win? If the will of the people is all that's important, how did the Empire conquer the galaxy in the first place?"

"To conquer and to rule are two very different things."

"And they seem as capable of keeping control as they were at taking control." Deadalus didn't know why he was so upset.

Flo shook her head in disagreement.

"I'm proof that they aren't. And Whiskey. And all the young kids that come to our performances. And it's not just here, there's discontent all through the galaxy. Right now, it's still mostly the artists and students, the ones who are the most sensitive. That's where it always starts. It'll spread. There's no way to stop it. You see, there's something in human beings that needs to be free. Not necessarily political freedom, or economic freedom, or even freedom of belief. It's a spirit inside, and I don't mean that religiously. People just won't put up with the oppression of their spirit. Sure, there's always a lot of compromising for the sake of security, but the need of the spirit to be free can never be fully stifled, and no government, no matter how strong, will ever be able to rule if it continually oppresses the spirit of the people."

Deadalus listened silently. The sincerity combined with her beauty, made her almost as persuasive talking as she was singing. He could glimpse something of the vision of her dream and there was something in it that moved him.

He could think of a thousand things that he knew about the secret workings of the Empire that seemed to refute her prophecy of its doom. But looking at her he didn't want to argue.

"Why don't you sing something?" he suggested rather suddenly. "Something nice. A love song."

She looked at him, surprised at his suggestion. Then her face flushed with anger.

"You stupid men are all the same! First you assume that a female doesn't know what she's talking about. But if any female proves that she does, that she has a brain, and is willing to think and discuss, you get put off and want to change the subject."

"No, no. That's not what I meant at all. It's just been a long day and I don't feel like arguing."

They stared at each other across the small table and Deadalus felt a physical awareness of her with his entire body. It was as if his entire skin had become sensually aware of her. Even if he closed his eyes, he would be able to describe her every movement, her every feature.

Across the room on the couch Whiskey stirred and groaned loudly in pain. Flo got up quickly and went over to him, sitting down on the edge of the couch next to him. Deadalus turned and watched her as she quieted him, checking his compresses and trying to make him comfortable. She sat, holding the young man's bandaged hand. Then in a very soft voice, her head bent and her eyes on the floor, she began singing.

It wasn't really a love song. It was more the kind of song that a mother would sing to soothe her child to sleep. It was filled with love and peace and comfort and that eternal assurance a mother gives her children that no matter what they do or how bad they are, she will still love them. The soft song didn't argue or deny any evil in the world, it just seemed to assert that in the balance between good and evil, love and hate, it was the better emotions that irrevocably won.

As Deadalus sat watching Flo and listening to her wonderful voice, he became extremely agitated. He was suddenly overcome with the awareness that his whole reason for being there was to kill. He could simply shoot Flo and Whiskey right here and his mission would be completed. He also realized that the longer he waited, the harder it would become. In the end he wouldn't be able to complete his mission, and the consequences of that were so great he was unable to think about them.

Flo's ideas about peaceful resistance were wrong. Just as she considered herself as proof that the Empire would eventually fall, Deadalus considered himself as proof that her methods would never win. She was too naive, too good-hearted, to be able to conceive how devious evil could be. She would never believe that the Empire would send someone to kill her, simply because the governor was in love with her and the governor needed to be brought into line. What would she say if he told her that his instructions had not been to simply kill her, but to kill her in a flamboyant manner?

The song came to an end and Deadalus stood, too agitated to be able to sit any longer. He couldn't take it anymore. He had to get away from here and try to think.

When the song finished, and Whiskey was once again under the power of the sedative, Flo stood and turned toward Deadalus.

"Don't go yet," she said.

"Yes, I have to."

She smiled. "But I still haven't proved to you that love overcomes all. And I saved my best argument for last."

Deadalus was so entranced by the look in her eyes that at first he didn't even notice that she had dropped her thin gown to the floor.

But eventually he did notice. Of course.

NINE

Deadalus stared at Flo, caught in a conflict of emotions. His training told him to get away quickly. His instincts told him to take the beautiful naked lady in his arms and give into the feelings that were welling inside.

Flo stood still, watching him and hesitantly waiting for some indication of his reaction. She balanced her weight on one leg, the other crossed behind her, her toes lightly on the floor. She reached back and untied her long hair, a motion which emphasized her firm breasts and hard, flat stomach.

Deadalus's eye followed the outline of her strong thighs, narrow hips, and smooth soft breasts and shoulders. He found that his mouth was suddenly dry. He swallowed with difficulty.

She shifted her weight and let her long dark hair cascade over her shoulders. The corners of her mouth turned down slightly as Deadalus continued to stand motionless, neither advancing nor retreating.

71

Deadalus noticed the slight frown and laughed out loud at himself.

"Caught me by surprise, Flo," he said, shaking his head and crossing the short distance between them.

She smiled at him as he put his hands on her shoulders, gently brushing her hair back. He looked into her face and again felt a wave of indecision.

"Are you sure you know what you're doing?" It was a question he had not asked a lady since he was a schoolkid.

In answer, she put her arms around his neck and pressed her lips to his.

The kiss started gently as their lips explored each other's. His mouth pressed harder on hers and she responded with equal passion. Then her mouth was open and he felt her moist tongue pressing up between his lips and into his mouth with sharp, quick thrusts. Finally she pulled back away from him far enough to speak.

"I have a bedroom, you know." Her breathless voice sounded slightly amused. "That sedative I gave Whiskey isn't foolproof."

Deadalus smiled and allowed her to lead him into the other room.

The bedroom was rather unusual and if Deadalus hadn't been trained to expect the unusual he might have been taken aback.

First of all, though Deadalus had noted that there was a regular security lock door that could be pulled out from the wall to separate the bedroom from the other room, Flo didn't use it. Instead she closed the doorway off with a curtain made out of something which resembled grains of rice strung together on magnetic thread. Though it would part easily when you pushed it, it immediately clung together forming a clothlike barrier.

The room itself was extremely small, only large enough for the bed and a mirrored cosmetic table, but at first glance it seemed enormous. The illusion of size was caused by the blue paint on the walls and ceiling, making them seem three-dimensional. You didn't get the feeling of looking at a flat surface. Instead, it seemed as if you were looking into the depths of space.

The bed was the most peculiar aspect of the whole room. It appeared to be a giant sponge. It was greenish-brown and about two-feet high, four-feet wide, and six-feet long.

Even in the most distracting of circumstances, Deadalus's mind automatically made note of these details. This was certainly the most distracting of circumstances.

Flo started unbuttoning his shirt but he stopped her, gently kissing her and pushing her down onto the bed. His preference for undressing himself was not one of undue modesty. He couldn't chance her stumbling across his weapons. Not only did he not wish discovery, but the least bit of carelessness could put a rather abrupt end to the evening. And a good portion of the city as well.

Her mouth was busy on his as he dropped his clothes on the floor near the head of the bed, and she did not notice as he concealed his gun within easy reach.

He kissed down her neck to her breasts, where her nipples stood firm and erect. She moaned loudly as he bit down, and her hands came alive on his body, stroking, probing, and caressing until neither of them could wait any longer.

For twenty minutes Deadalus was able to forget about who he was and what he had come for. But when they finally lay together, quiet, sweaty, and contented, his mind once again filled with the worry of his mission.

Flo sat up, leaning on her elbow, and with one delicate finger traced the line of his mouth, looking at him thoughtfully.

"I don't even know who you are," she said softly.

He smiled and kissed her finger.

"Who are you? What are you doing on Eurydice? What is it that you want?" Her voice was still a whisper but her eyes showed an insistence that he couldn't avoid.

He looked at her, feeling something move inside him that he had never felt before, something he couldn't explain. He automatically started to tell her the cover story about being a salesman, but stopped. That cover wasn't good anymore. Even if she was willing to believe it, he wouldn't be able to lie to her.

He wanted to tell her the truth, tell her that he was a secret agent for the Empirical police, tell her that he had been sent here to kill her. He wanted to tell her everything about himself that he had never told anyone before. It suddenly seemed of the utmost importance that she know exactly who and what he was and that she accept him for that and not for anything else.

Deadalus struggled for words. He strained to give utterance to all the secrets he held inside of him. Flo's eyes widened with concern as his face reflected the battle that was going on inside him. He opened his mouth, but no words came out. All he could manage was a sound that was half-groan and half-sigh of defeat. His training went too deep. He couldn't reveal his identity to her. Not yet.

"I don't know," he said finally in a low voice. "I guess I'm not who I thought I was. I guess I don't know who I am."

She leaned over and kissed him quick and hard.

"I'm sorry, I didn't mean to get you so upset. You don't have to tell me if you don't want to. I was just thinking though, if you were going to be staying on Eurydice for a while I might be able to get the governor to call off the police. About the brawl, I mean."

"No, Flo. There's a little more to it than that. There's a little more than the brawl for the governor to be upset with me for."

"Do you want me to see what I can do, anyway?"

Deadalus smiled. "There's nothing you can do, believe me. The best thing would be to never let them know that you know me. If they ask you about the fight in the bar, just tell them that you never saw me before and that I disappeared afterwards. Don't get involved. Besides, I'm not really worried about the police. I'm not going to be on Eurydice that much longer."

Flo looked at him quietly, her dark eyes soft with emotion. Then suddenly she smiled slyly.

"Let's not talk about all that. I know something better to do."

She leaned over and bit his ear.

An hour later Deadalus awoke from the light doze he had fallen into. His sleeping mind had picked up some danger signal and brought him instantly awake. He lay perfectly motionless, trying to see what it was that had woken him up.

He was lying on his back with Flo asleep on his right shoulder. He couldn't have moved quickly even if he wanted to. He lay still and listened.

There was a sound from the doorway.

With his left hand he reached into his pile of clothes and found his gun.

The corner of the curtain was gently pulled open.

Deadalus tensed his body, ready to fling himself up and aside. His finger was on the trigger button ready to start firing. He was a good shot even with his left hand. Besides, the doorway was only a few feet away.

The hand that cracked open the curtain had a large bandage on it. Deadalus could just make out the form of Whiskey's bandaged face.

Deadalus relaxed, but still kept his grip on the gun, waiting. He was not sure what was going to happen.

Whiskey stared into the room for a long moment. Then he moved away. The curtain made a soft click as it pulled shut.

Deadalus still waited, listening and thinking. After a minute he could hear sounds from the other room, and then the sound of a bottle on the table. Deadalus came to a decision.

He gently pulled his arm out from under Flo, careful not to wake her, and pulled on his clothes. He made a quick check of all his weapons and then pushed through the curtain into the other room.

Whiskey was sitting on the far side of the table. In front of him was a bottle, a drinking glass, and two knives. Deadalus carefully studied the young man's face as he crossed over to the table. It was hard and determined. Whatever it was that Whiskey was planning to do, he wasn't going to be talked out of it.

"How do you feel?" Deadalus asked, sitting down.

Whiskey stared at him, silent. After a moment the young man shrugged in reply.

"Well, you sure found the trouble you were looking for in that bar," Deadalus continued as if he didn't notice the young man's angry silence. "I'm surprised that you're up already."

Whiskey took a sip from his drink.

"I don't like you," the young man said in a low, constricted voice.

Deadalus shrugged and poured himself a drink. He could see what was coming, but he had learned enough about the young man to know that he wasn't going to be able to reason with him when he was in this type of mood.

"Who asked you to get involved anyway?" Whiskey said angrily, as if he couldn't stop speaking. "Why did you come here? Asking your questions, insinuating yourself into here. I figure you're one of the governor's men."

"That's a rather surprising conclusion. How did you come to that?"

"Because there's no other reason why Flo

78

would sleep with someone like you," he spat out.

Deadalus finished his drink and set the glass gently on the table.

"Don't waste my time trying to fabricate an excuse," Deadalus replied evenly. "If you're planning to challenge me, get to it. I've got other things to do."

Whiskey finished his drink quickly and then pushed the two knives to the center of the table for Deadalus to choose one.

Deadalus smiled thinly.

"Why don't you keep them both, kid? You're going to need them."

Instantly, as if by magic, Deadalus's own knife was in his hand.

Whiskey was taken aback by the sudden appearance of the blade, but only for the slightest of moments. He quickly grabbed the knives off the table and jumped to his feet.

Deadalus stood and backed away from the table, allowing Whiskey to come around into the open area of the room. Deadalus watched the young man as he moved, noting where Whiskey balanced his weight, which muscles he seemed to favor, and how he held the knives.

Deadalus feinted down to his left and then leaped into the air, spinning around and grabbing the young man around the chest with his legs, pinning Whiskey's arms and throwing him heavily to the ground.

He held Whiskey motionless, pinned to the floor, and pressed the flat side of his blade against the young man's throat. Whiskey's teeth were clenched, feeling the cool metal against his jugular and waiting for the final slash that was sure to come. Deadalus let him sweat for a minute.

"Do it, damn you!" Whiskey hissed at him through his clenched teeth. "Or don't you have the nerve?"

Deadalus laughed. "I'd just have to bandage you up again? No thanks."

He let go and hopped to his feet.

Whiskey lay for a moment, breathing heavily. Then, in one smooth motion he rolled over and came to his feet charging at Deadalus.

Deadalus dove under Whiskey's slashing blades and kicked the young man's feet from under him. As the young man fell, Deadalus tapped Whiskey's stomach with the side of his knife, almost as if playing a child's game of tag.

Whiskey came up slowly this time. His face was pale and his mouth was set into a thin hard line.

"Alright, had enough?" Deadalus asked.

"You've proven your point." The young man's voice was low and he spoke with great difficulty. "Now you'd better quit playing games and kill me. Because if you don't, I'm going to kill you."

"Deadalus?" Flo's sleepy voice called from the bedroom.

"Sorry, I can't oblige you, Whiskey," Deadalus said.

He did a quick double feint then leaped in

the air spinning, and brought his foot down on the side of Whiskey's head.

With a small moan, the young man crumbled to the floor, unconscious.

Deadalus picked him up and carried him over to the couch. He lay the young man down comfortably and readjusted some of the bandages which had come loose during the fight.

"Deadalus? Whiskey?" Flo's voice was louder and Deadalus could hear her getting out of bed.

Quickly and silently he picked up the knives that Whiskey had dropped, put them on the table, and left the apartment.

ELEVEN

There was a whir and a buzz, a red light came on, and the machine rejected Deadalus's card. He stared uncomprehendingly, wondering what had suddenly happened to his credit. Then he realized that he had placed his card in backward. He started to reinsert it properly but then shrugged and turned away. If he couldn't get the card in right he didn't need another drink anyway.

Deadalus looked across the hotel lobby where the thick sunlight of Therminous came in through the clear-rock door. The entire building was built from different kinds of stone, all natural to the planet. The large doors and windows were made from thick slices of highly polished quartz and the floor was of leaded marble.

Deadalus hadn't come here to admire architectural grandeur. He had come to get some thinking done, yet it seemed the more he thought, the less he was sure about his situation.

Deadalus stared at the sunlight and considered going somewhere, but there was nowhere to go. He turned and crossed through the elaborate indoor garden and down the short hallway to his room entrance.

One end of the room was made from the same transparent quartz and looked onto the garden. Deadalus rolled back the curtain and sat down, staring at the greenery.

He had had no trouble getting off Eurydice. He simply returned to his apartment where, as he expected, the police were awaiting him. Deadalus had relieved the three men of their senses, their weapons, and his luggage. He caught the next shuttle for Therminous and had checked in here under another name. They would be able to trace him, of course, but from his experience with local police, it would take a couple days, and that was enough time for Deadalus to decide what he was going to do.

He couldn't go ahead with his mission as planned, that was clear enough. Even if he wasn't emotionally involved with Flo, the injustice and brutality of what he had been assigned to do sickened him. This disgust for the methods of the secret police had been growing in him for a longtime and had only begun to surface. In the past, he had kept in mind the intent of the agency and the necessity of such force. How else was one going to keep someone like Governor Washba in line, for instance? But now Deadalus could clearly see that the Empire had no intentions of trying to make the government in the V-Two sector just and humane. They merely wanted the governor to be more cooperative with them so they could get what they wanted. They didn't care how he kept order on his two planets. The disillusionment that he felt over the entire system, which he had been an intricate part of, was so complete that Deadalus wondered how he had ever been fool enough to believe in it in the first place.

Deadalus wasn't willing to give in. Maybe there was something that he could do to change things. At least, he should try to rectify the case at hand.

He knew what should be done; he should go after the governor directly. Washba was not only the source of the problem from the Empire's standpoint, he was also a great problem to the people he ruled. Since the governors were considered the local representatives of the Empire, the people considered that the governor's actions were the will of the larger government. The people blamed the Empire for the things that Governor Washba did. As long as he was allowed to get away with it, the Empire was at fault.

If Washba was removed or brought under stiff control, not only would the Empirical government solve its problem, but they would also gain the gratitude of the people in this sector. Well, maybe not all the people. The few rich and powerful, who were benefiting by Washba's policies certainly would not be happy, but they were only a handful and would be outbalanced by the masses who would pledge a new allegiance to the Empire.

Deadalus didn't have the authority to go

after the governor. Agents for the secret police were given complete authority to use any means that they deemed necessary in completing their mission. What Deadalus wanted to do was to actually change his mission, and that, he supposed, would be punishable by death. He really couldn't say. He had never heard of such a situation before.

What he was going to do was contact Chief Hissler and see if he couldn't talk him into changing his mind and giving him permission to do what Deadalus thought necessary. If that failed, and Deadalus had his doubts about Hissler's cooperation, he could insist on an audience before the board to plead his case. Though that was what the board was supposed to be for, Deadalus had never heard of such a thing happening.

Deadalus wasn't even sure how to contact the chief. You weren't supposed to contact the office until your mission was completed and you were back on Earth. Unless, of course, you failed. But the only failures that Deadalus had ever heard of were the cases where the agent turned up dead or disappeared altogether.

Deadalus hadn't failed at his mission. He hadn't even tried. And he knew that there was no way that he could go through with it as planned. Even if it meant his death.

Political beliefs aside, there was no way that he could kill Flo. The way he felt about her was something that he had never felt before, and it was more powerful than even his drive for self-survival. He would kill himself before he would kill her.

That was the most extreme solution. First he would try everything he could to protect her and make sure that the chief didn't just send another agent out to complete the mission that Deadalus couldn't. He would have to contact the chief and find out exactly where he stood.

Deadalus decided that he needed another drink after all.

The private viewing screen turned beige, then filled with static as Deadalus punched in the code number for the chief's office. Deadalus sat in his hotel room as patiently as he could while his call worked its way through the marvels of communication technology and its maze of connections. Finally the signal did manage to make it through and was answered by the chief's secretary.

Deadalus saw the look of surprise on her face.

"May I help you?" she asked, careful not to use his name. This was supposed to be a secure line, but from this far there was no line that was truly secure.

"I'd like to talk to the boss."

"I'm sorry, he doesn't receive any calls. Can I take a message?"

Deadalus made the sign with his hand to indicate that all was clear on his end of the line, a supposed precaution against agents being forced to try and contact the chief.

The secretary looked as if she was about to ask him something, then decided against it and turned and buzzed the chief's office. There was a moment as he heard her talking to Hissler off screen and then she turned back to him, her face showing her honest concern.

"He'll take your call now. Is there anything else I can do for you?"

This last question was not part of any security ritual but rather an expression of her own concern.

Deadalus winked and blew her a kiss.

"I'll let you know, honey," he said with a smile.

She returned his smile and then her face was replaced by the cold craggy features of the chief.

Hissler stared into the viewing screen, his hard features unmoving. He waited for Deadalus to explain.

"I seem to have a problem," Deadalus began, somewhat hesitant.

Hissler grunted expressively.

Deadalus chose his words carefully in case the call was being monitored by someone on Therminous, or in any of the connecting way-stations between him and Earth.

"I contacted the potential buyers without any problem."

"And did you sell them the bill of goods?" the chief snapped, grimacing at Deadalus's choice of metaphor.

"No. I had contact with another party which I feel would be a better sell."

Hissler frowned and turned away from the screen. There was a few moments of static, then the chief's face came back on.

"Alright, Captain. I just ran a trace on this line and it's clear, at least for the moment. You want to tell me what the hell you're talking about?"

Deadalus noted the professionalism in Hissler's voice. That always signaled trouble. What did he expect anyway? Deadalus shrugged slightly and relaxed into his chair.

"I've observed the situation quite closely and have concluded that the mission is wrong as planned. Killing the artists would not achieve the objective. It would push the governor to becoming even more difficult, and it could very well strengthen his position. He is abhorred by the people, quite justly I might add. But if he takes the side of the slain artists the people would most likely rally behind him. I would like to use my authority as the agent in charge to go after the governor directly."

Hissler's face had become quite red by this time.

"Have you done anything on this line? If you've done anything . . ."

"I thought it best to contact you first," Deadalus interrupted.

"Damn right!" the chief snapped back. "That is completely beyond the realm of your authority. You don't know anything. We know all about what's going on in the V-Two sector. You haven't observed anything that wasn't taken into our calculations."

Hissler was yelling so loudly that Deadalus reached up and turned down the volume on his screen.

"I wasn't assuming any authority," Deadalus replied calmly. "That's why I called."

Hissler stared at him through the screen in disbelief.

"You telling me that you called to get permission to change your assigned mission because you don't like it?"

"Because it's wrong."

"Well, you don't got it! You hear me? You complete your mission as assigned! Because if you don't, if you do anything unauthorized in regard to the governor, I'm going to have you strung up so high you're never coming down! You hear me, Captain?"

"I request an audience before the board, then."

"You aren't getting an audience with anyone until you get your damn mission completed!"

"I will not complete the mission as assigned! I have a right to bring my complaint before the board and have them arbitrate!" Deadalus's voice was as loud and angry as Hissler's.

"Arbitrate? In the middle of an assignment? Are you out of your mind? You complete your mission, as assigned. Any failure to do so will be considered treason. Do you hear me, Captain Deadalus? You disobey direct orders and you'll have your audience with the board, alright. I'll personally see to it!"

"I quit."

Deadalus's voice was so quiet it caught the chief by surprise.

"What?"

"I said I quit. I resign. I'm sick and tired of the whole thing. I hereby resign from the secret police."

Hissler had become absolutely silent, staring at Deadalus in disbelief. The silence drew out to a full minute, and then another. Finally the chief spoke and now his voice was level and professional.

"Alright, Captain. Let's not be hasty. Why don't you come back to Earth and we'll talk this over? Your effectiveness where you are is obviously compromised anyway."

"Will I be able to bring my case before the board?"

"Yes," Hissler sighed heavily. "You will have your audience with the board—if you still find it necessary."

The chief turned away from the screen and briefly consulted a computer display.

"We have a starship returning from a nearby sector. I'll have him swing by and pick you up. It will save some time over those damn commercial liners. Captain Wok is in charge of the ship. Do you know him?"

"Yes."

"Good. That always makes it easier. Any problem getting to the spaceport by mid-morning tomorrow?"

"Tomorrow? That soon? No, I can be there if I start right away."

"Alright. Any further questions?"

Deadalus shook his head and turned off the screen. At the last moment, just before the screen went blank, Deadalus saw a peculiar smile flicker across the chief's stony features.

Chief Hissler sat in front of the blank screen and drummed his fingers lightly on the desk top. Then, consulting the computer terminal, he punched some numbers and waited.

"Let me speak to Captain Wok," he said when the screen came to life. The agent on the other end complied immediately.

"Chief Hissler." The captain on the starship looked somewhat disconcerted by this unusual contact from the chief.

"Captain, I've got a job for you. You are to change courses immediately and head for the V-Two sector. How soon can you get there?"

The captain turned and checked on his shipboard computer.

"Approximately a day and a half, sir."

"Good. You are to proceed there as quickly as possible. You will pick up Captain Deadalus at the spaceport. He'll be waiting."

"Yes, sir."

"You will then proceed into free space. Once there you will terminate Captain Deadalus."

The chief was watching the man on the screen very closely and was therefore able to see the captain's right hand move slightly off the armrest and push a lever. Hissler smiled grimly to himself. The agent had just started taping this conversation. Strictly against regulations, of course. The captain was smart enough to know that he would need something to protect himself with. Hissler decided that Wok was a good man to use for this mission.

"Excuse me, sir," the captain said. "I seem to be having trouble with my reception. Could you repeat that last instruction?"

"You are to kill Captain Deadalus. Understood?"

"Yes, sir." The captain's face was set, revealing no emotion.

"I told Deadalus that you were going to be picking him up tomorrow morning because I didn't want him running around loose for a day and a half. So in about six hours you are going to have to call the spaceport and leave a message that you are having mechanical difficulty, but that you should be underway shortly. Every few hours you will call in saying the same thing. I want to keep him waiting at the spaceport, is that understood?"

"Yes, sir."

"Before you kill him, you are to try to get some information from him. Start by saying that you were ordered to get a full report on his mission."

"Yes sir. What kind of information am I to be looking for?"

"It's uncertain. Captain Deadalus has threatened to resign under peculiar circumstances. You are to find out exactly why."

"What if the captain resists divulging the information?"

Hissler was surprised by the question at first. The captain knew very well what he was to do. Then the chief remembered that the conversation was being taped. Wok was taking every precaution to keep well-covered if something fouled up.

"You are to use every available means to get him to talk, Captain Wok. The information may be extremely important to the welfare of the Empirical government."

Hissler waited a moment to make sure that there was no misunderstanding.

"Deadalus may be on his guard, Captain. You are to proceed with utmost caution. I don't think I have to tell you how dangerous he is. I feel I must advise you, for your own well-being as well as for the success of this mission. Don't try anything fancy with Deadalus. Don't try to take him on by yourself. Use every bit of force that's available to you. Deadalus is deadly. He may be the most dangerous single man loose in the galaxy."

THIRTEEN

"Captain Deadalus?"

Deadalus turned. The man who addressed him was short, slightly plump, and nearly bald.

"Ah, Captain Wok. You made it after all." Deadalus was unable to completely mask his weariness.

"Sorry about the delay," Wok said, shaking Deadalus's outstretched hand. "Just one of those unpredictable breakdowns."

"Well, I trust you've gotten it fixed."

"We certainly hope so, Deadalus."

Captain Wok turned and introduced Deadalus to the five crew members who had accompanied him into the landing craft.

The five men were members of the secret police, though of the lowest rank. Only the best of the agents achieved the rank of captain, and then only after years of work and a great deal of success.

Deadalus was surprised by the number of men Wok had brought with him in the landing craft. Three was the customary number of people in a landing craft, and that was merely precautionary. One man could easily pilot the craft. You could always fit as many people as you wanted as payload, the entire crew of a starship if the situation called for it. And Deadalus perceived from the attitude of the crew and Wok as they returned to the craft that they seemed to be expecting some trouble. Perhaps they had received word to watch for the local police. Or maybe they had just completed an extremely dangerous mission, and Deadalus knew that cautious habits were hard to break.

The crew, including Captain Wok, were dressed in a uniform bearing the insignia of a merchant shipping company.

There was little conversation as they took off in the shuttle and headed back toward the ship. The crew worked together smoothly, each man doing his job without being told. After they were safely away from the planet, Deadalus closed his eyes to rest.

He was extremely weary from the long wait in the spaceport. He had spent nearly two days expecting to be picked up in a few hours. Always the calls about the mechanical problems and that he'd have to wait longer. It wasn't the waiting which was so bad, the spaceport had every accommodation possible. So much time was being wasted that it bothered Deadalus and wore him down. If he had known in the beginning that he would have to wait that long, he could have put the time to good use. But he couldn't leave the spaceport because the ship was supposedly going to be there soon.

Now they had finally come and he was on his way back to Earth. He was really uncertain what awaited him there. There was something in that last glimpse of the chief, that odd flicker of a smile, that bothered Deadalus. There was something at the back of his mind that just couldn't quite work its way out. He had tried to think of it but had finally given up, deciding that he'd have to wait until he got back to Earth to find out what the situation was.

He woke up as they approached docking with the starship. He looked up at the pilot's screen, which showed the image of the secret police starship, one of the most effective fighting machines ever developed. Only the eyes of someone who had depended on it for his life could find any sort of beauty in the structure. Deadalus loved it.

The starship was round like a ball. Its surface was a dull gray due to the anti-radar coating, and was pocked with evenly spaced jets. When you got right on its surface you could see all the various weapons and surveillance equipment which studded the surface wherever the jets were not.

In the hands of a skillful captain and sharp crew, the secret police starship was virtually undefeatable. It could move in any direction and could change courses instantly, since there was no front or back or top or bottom. An opponent had no way to determine which direction it was going next, and, with the immense speeds that it was capable of, it was never in the same spot for long. It carried every sort of conceivable weapon and could, all by itself, destroy an entire planet.

There were, for political reasons, very few of them. The army had no starships, and was extremely jealous. They had managed to get the opponents of the secret police to keep a tight hold on the pursestrings, strictly limiting the number of ships that the secret police could build.

The docking maneuver was done automatically and there was little for the crew in the landing craft to worry about. Once inside, Deadalus was thankfully shown to a cabin where he could freshen up and get some rest before the evening meal.

As Deadalus was preparing to shower, one of the crew members came in.

"The captain said to make sure that you check in everything but shipboard weapons, sir."

Deadalus was a bit surprised. It was customary to lock away all explosives and projectile weapons when going into action. You didn't want one of your crew members to blow a hole in the hull. It was a precaution which was usually taken only if you expected to be meeting trouble.

"You expecting some sort of action?" Deadalus asked while getting out his weapons.

"Captain didn't say, sir. Will you be wanting to come down to the armory and get a shipboard laser?"

"No, I was just about to shower. I'll get it when I come down for the meal."

Deadalus was extremely uneasy while showering. He was tired and on edge, and to be left with nothing but his knife, no matter how momentarily, seemed to compound his uneasy feeling. And there was that damn smile on the chief's face when the chief shouldn't have been smiling.

After his shower, Deadalus laid down for a few hours of restless sleep.

Deadalus was awakened by the buzzer that signaled the evening meal. He dressed, still feeling somewhat groggy and tired, as if he couldn't quite wake up. He noticed the emptiness of the corridors as he walked, and when he did finally meet one of the crew he asked him about it.

"How many men are on this starship? Seems awfully quiet."

"We've only fourteen men, sir."

"Fourteen! That's just above minimum."

"Yes, sir."

Deadalus thought to himself as they entered the mess hall. It took twelve men to fly the starship, that was the bare minimum. To have only fourteen was calling it pretty close. Deadalus wondered what kind of mission Wok could have been on. He certainly must have started out with more than fourteen men. No wonder they all seemed nervous and on edge.

Deadalus found his curiosity peaked, but it was considered poor form to ask another agent about his mission so he refrained from further questions.

Deadalus got his food and sat down at the

large, circular table. Six of the crew not counting Wok were eating, the other seven would be on duty.

There was little conversation during the meal, everyone seemed distracted. The obvious edginess of the crew added to Deadalus's own, and he was lost in his worries about what he was going to say to the board and what the chief was thinking.

The meal over, the crew members milled around trying to postpone going back on duty. Deadalus got up and excused himself to the captain, thinking that he'd feel better in his cabin. Wok stood up with him.

"Um, this is rather awkward, Deadalus," Wok said uneasily. "But I've been instructed by the chief to get a full report from you on your mission. I didn't want to, but the chief was awfully mad and I thought it best not to argue."

Deadalus looked at Wok for a moment in complete puzzlement. The request made no sense whatsoever. Why would the chief want him to give a report to Wok? Even if that were the common practice, which it definitely was not, it wouldn't be suitable at all in this case.

Deadalus sensed a motion behind him.

Suddenly the chief's odd smile made sense.

Without thinking but acting on instinct alone, Deadalus leaped in the air, spinning. His arm was a blur of motion and his knife buried itself to the hilt in the throat of the crew member behind him, even before the unfortunate man could aim the gun he was holding.

Someone else fired at him as he came down

with both feet full on the side of Wok's head. Wok's head whipped back and the captain dropped the gun he held as he crumbled to the floor.

Deadalus dove for the gun, but he knew he didn't stand a chance. He wasn't going to beat seven trained agents who had their guns drawn and were all dead shots.

Two shots hit Deadalus even before he could complete the thought.

FOURTEEN

Deadalus's consciousness fought the thick black murk that was trying to smother it. The warning system that was trained into his nerves was going full force. He had to open his eyes. His life depended on getting the gun and defending himself.

Slowly the consciousness fought its way to the surface. Agonizingly he opened one eye.

He was alone in a cabin. He was bound hand and foot. They weren't going to kill him. Not right at the moment at least.

Gratefully Deadalus let his conscious spin back into the darkness.

The next time Deadalus woke up it was easier. His mouth was bone dry and his body stank with stale sweat. He opened his eyes and looked around. He was still alone in a cabin, lying prone on an acceleration couch. His hands were bound behind him and his feet were bound to the bottom of the couch. He was naked.

He closed his eyes and concentrated on clear-

105

ing his mind of the painful buzzing that filled it. He quickly went over the details of the situation.

Chief Hissler was going to have him assassinated, that was clear enough. It was an extreme reaction on the Chief's part, though logical, and Deadalus was surprised that he had not considered it before. What wasn't clear was why he was still alive.

He had been shot by an electric stun gun, not the lasers which were usually carried on board. If he had been shot by a laser he wouldn't have the throbbing that he had in his head. He wouldn't have a head. So evidently the crew had been instructed to just knock him out, not kill him. But why? They were going to have to kill him sooner or later after this. What was it that they hoped to gain by waiting? What was it that Wok had said about a report? Maybe the chief thought that Deadalus had some useful information which he was holding back on. Maybe they just wanted some information before they killed him.

Maybe the chief had specified a slow and painful death or maybe the chief wanted to do it himself.

Deadalus looked around, trying to get his bearings. From the ache in his muscles he had been lying unconscious for a number of hours. The cabin he was in was just an ordinary crew cabin, empty except for the ship furnishings. Deadalus tried to sit up but he was strapped to the couch. He was about to see if he could undue the straps when the cabin door opened.

Two crew members came in, their guns out and ready. Deadalus noted that this time they were using lasers. To his mild surprise Captain Wok was behind the agents.

Around the captain's neck was a firm splint so he couldn't turn his head. Deadalus's kick had evidently caused some damage, though not as much as Deadalus thought he had done.

The two guards took up positions along the far wall, their guns aimed at Deadalus. The captain advanced and stood in front of the couch, frowning down at Deadalus.

"Can I have some water?" Deadalus asked hoarsely.

Wok seemed to want to ignore his request, then turned and went over to the wall and brought Deadalus some water. He raised the couch so that Deadalus was in a sitting position and held the glass for Deadalus to drink from.

"So what's going on here, Wok?" Deadalus asked after he was through drinking.

The captain's face showed that he was fighting more than physical pain. Wok was obviously upset by the whole business.

"I've been instructed to get a full and complete report from you about what happened on your mission. Chief Hissler is particularly interested in information dealing with your sudden desire to quit the agency. He's instructed me to use any means to get this information."

Deadalus stared at him silently, trying to think of how he could use this situation to his advantage. Captain Wok grew uneasy under the other's cold stare.

"Listen, Deadalus, you know I don't like doing this. Though you do have a way of making it easier," he added gingerly touching his neck brace.

"Think of yourself as lucky, Wok. I had meant to kill you. I must be slipping up."

Anyone but another police agent would have gotten angry by Deadalus's reply. Wok smiled.

"You know the situation as well as I do, Deadalus. Why don't you just save us a lot of unpleasantness and give me whatever information it is that the chief is after."

Deadalus was about to reply quite honestly that he didn't have any information whatsoever, but then he caught the glimmer of an idea. He stared for a moment at the other captain and then nodded his head toward the two agents standing guard.

"Get rid of the two rookies, Wok, and maybe we can talk."

"No way, Deadalus. We had you by surprise seven to one and you broke my neck and killed one of my men. I'm not going to trust you alone."

"But I'm bound hand and foot and strapped into a goddamn chair and you know I don't have any weapons up my sleeve because I don't have any sleeves on at all! Listen, they can stand right outside the door. I just want them out of earshot so we can talk freely. Come on, Captain."

The last remark was a slap at Wok's pride as a top secret police agent and it had its calculated effect. Wok came over and, making sure that Deadalus's bonds and straps were tight, motioned for the two guards to leave. He then drew out his own gun and stood against the far wall, a safe twenty feet away from Deadalus.

"Alright, talk."

"OK. This is the way I see it. You're going to kill me one way or the other. If I give you all the information it won't do me any good, you'll just kill me sooner. If I don't give you the information freely we know there are techniques which will drag it out of me no matter how hard I try to resist, and all I would gain from that would be a few hours of very painful existence. So my choices seem to be to either give you the information freely and get killed straight out, or else to have the information dragged painfully out of me and then be killed."

"So what do you plan to do, Deadalus?" Wok asked, remaining noncommital.

"Well, there's one other possibility. It's a long shot, I know. But as you'll agree, I don't really have much to lose by trying. I want you to join up with me against the agency."

Wok grunted disgustedly. "Who are you trying to fool?"

"Think about it a minute, Wok. You know that I've been one of the very top agents for a number of years, and that I've received all the benefits of that position. I know as well as anyone alive exactly how powerful the secret police really are. Do you think that I would join up with someone else if I wasn't certain that there was some chance of success? And don't you think that I would stick with the agency unless I knew that I could get better benefits somewhere else, benefits so great that they far outweighed the trouble it took to get them?"

Wok thought about it a moment. His puzzled expression showed that he recognized the logic in what Deadalus was saying.

"What guarantee would you have that I'd keep my word, Deadalus? I'm certainly not going to let you loose until you've given me all the information anyway. And then I could still just as easily kill you."

"I know, I know, it's risky from my standpoint. Everything's risky from where I'm sitting. Here's the way we'll work it. I'll give you enough information about what's going on for you to be able to see both sides of the game. I'm not going to give you any names, I'll just tell you enough so that you can make up your mind. If you decide to throw in with me then I'll give you the rest of the information."

"And if I decide not to join you?"

"Then you'll have to force the rest out of me. And we know that that's not an easy task. Don't think that you can kill me and still join the organization behind me. Believe me, even with all the information, you could never get in without me."

Wok thought for awhile, his eyes narrowed, trying to determine if Deadalus really was desperate or if he was just offering a gambit. Then he shrugged.

"It seems that I don't have anything to lose at this point. Alright, you tell me what you're going to tell me and then I'll decide whether to join you or not."

Deadalus felt his heart quicken but was careful to keep his face expressionless.

"That's all I want, Wok. Just be willing to consider it. I think that what I tell you will be strong enough to make up your mind for you.

"Basically and simply—an antimatter bomb has been developed."

Wok's face registered his amazement.

"Impossible!"

"You know it's not impossible. The Empire has been trying to come up with such a bomb for the past decade. I've even heard reports that we came close a couple of times. Now it's been developed, but not by the Empire. Now I'm no technician so I wouldn't have been able to understand the workings of it even if they had told me, and you can rest assured that they didn't. So I don't know if its development was a matter of luck or genius or what. Five of them have been built and are in the hands of a small group of people who are ready and willing to use them if they have to."

"Why would they ever use them? Wouldn't they destroy the galaxy?"

"Evidently not. It turns out that the antimatter is neutralized by the positive matter that it destroys, although there is quite a bit of matter destroyed before neutralization. Each of the five bombs built have enough antimatter to destroy roughly a quarter of the galaxy."

"Who are these people and how do they plan to use the bombs?"

111

"I'm not going to tell you their names. Not that it would do you much good anyways. There's no way of destroying the group without setting off the bombs, but the group doesn't want to use the bombs. They figure that the mere threat will be enough to get what they want. And if they are forced to back up the threat, one explosion would be enough to drive everyone left into submission."

"I can believe that. But what is it that they want, Deadalus?"

"Just the same thing that everyone else wants. They would rather rule than be ruled."

The two men sat silent, their eyes watching every muscle twitch and gesture of the other.

"Well, what about it, Wok?"

"I'll have to check your story out before I decide." The captain spoke carefully.

Deadalus nodded. "That shouldn't take too long. I'd appreciate it if you'd hurry. These bonds aren't the most comfortable."

Wok considered for a minute longer and Deadalus held his breath. Then the captain turned stiffly and left the cabin.

Once alone, Deadalus worked fast. He knew he didn't have much time. Five minutes if he was very lucky.

Of course Wok had no intention of turning traitor. He had merely agreed to listen in hopes of making his job a little easier. The story that Deadalus had handed him was ridiculous, but then. Wok had expected the truth to be outlandish. Now the captain had gone to contact the chief and see if the chief would be satisfied

with the tale. The task of forcing inform...
out of someone, especially someone with Deadalus's training, was an ordeal that Wok wasn't
going to do unless he had to.

Undoing the two straps that held him against
the couch was not a great problem, despite the
fact that his hands were bound together behind
him. The straps had a quick release mechanism
on the buckles, designed for shipboard emer-
gencies. Deadalus had to twist far enough
around so that he could reach the mechanism.

With the straps loose, Deadalus set to work
on the binding that held his feet. He would
have preferred his hands free, but he could feel
that the binding around his wrists was the old-
fashioned plastic type. They were simple but
very efficient and it would take him much too
long to get out of them.

Someone had made the mistake of binding
Deadalus's feet with a new sophisticated binding that had a complicated electronic locking
device. For all its expense and sophistication, it
was much less efficient than the old-fashioned
kind.

Deadalus had never seen a lock he couldn't
pick, and he was very familiar with this type.
The only problem was that his hands were
bound behind him. Not only did he have to
nearly break his back in order to reach his feet,
but he couldn't watch what he was doing,
which slowed him down greatly.

Deadalus worked frantically, expecting for
the door to open at any moment and for Wok to
come in and burn his head off. Not that there

was really much of an option. Whatever happened it was obvious that Wok was committed to killing him.

Deadalus considered his chances of getting out alive to be impossible. His struggle to fight back and do all that he could was sheer instinct and training.

The electronic lock at last snapped open and Deadalus unwound the bonds from around his feet. It was a thin, flexible cable, about five-feet long, and had the heavy locking mechanism on one end. Deadalus decided that it would make a good weapon. At least, it would have to be good enough, he didn't have time to look for anything else.

He sat on the couch and put the straps back around him, this time without latching them. He held the coiled cable in his hands behind his back.

His only possible chance would be if Wok came back in alone. If he brought the two guards back with him, Deadalus might as well give up. Taking on Wok would be impossible enough.

Wok had a gun and use of both hands. Wok, like Deadalus, was an expertly trained fighter. Deadalus, on the other hand, had his hands bound behind his back and only a makeshift weapon. He did have the advantage of surprise, though that was only a small advantage against a trained agent on his guard. Wok's movements would be hampered by his neck brace.

The only real advantage on Deadalus's side was that he would be taking the attack and would therefore have one chance to control the course of action of the fight. Fighting someone who had studied the same training did have a good side; Deadalus would merely have to pretend that he was fighting himself and he would know what Wok was about to do.

Hopefully.

The door slid open. Every muscle in Deadalus's body tensed.

FIFTEEN

Wok stood in the doorway. He seemed to hesitate, then he took a step forward. The door slid
shut behind him, the two guards still outside.
Wok's gun was in his hand. He took another
step toward Deadalus.

Deadalus sprung into the air like a coiled
spring.

Fights are rarely won by single blows.
Usually it is a combination of blows that does
the trick. It was a matter of predicting which
way your opponent would move in response to
the first blow, and then getting the second
blow there before him.

The normal reaction to Deadalus's flying attack would be to drop back to avoid his feet,
which were drawn up in preparation for a kick.
But Deadalus had figured that what he would
do if he was in Wok's spot would be to duck
forward and under, coming up behind. There
were a number of reasons for this. One, the wall
was too close behind Wok to drop back suffi-
ciently, and, if there was to be more than one

117

attack, it would be a disadvantage to have your back to the wall. Ducking under would reverse the situation. Another reason was if he did get caught by the feet while ducking under, there would be less power to the blow if it was received on the end of the forward momentum. A third reason would be that dropping back would be the expected response. And it was better to do anything other than the expected.

Deadalus's success rested on the gamble that Wok would do what he himself would do in this situation. While he leaped, Deadalus swung the cable under him toward the spot where Wok's head would be if he tried ducking under. It was a poor way to fight. It was too risky. If Wok did anything other than that one response Deadalus was going to end up cut to pieces by the laser gun. But Deadalus didn't have a lot of choice.

What did happen was not exactly what Deadalus had planned.

Wok did duck, but much much quicker than Deadalus had anticipated. It was almost as if Wok had himself predicted Deadalus's attack and had prepared for it. As Wok ducked and turned he caught sight of the cable out of the corner of his eye and instinctively moved to dodge it while firing his gun at Deadalus at the same time. If the fight had been decided on skill, Deadalus would have lost.

But Deadalus didn't lose. The deciding factor was luck.

In trying to dodge the cable, Wok failed to take in the restrictions caused by the brace on his neck, which he had only been wearing for a number of hours. Thus the heavy mechanism on the end of the cable which had been intended to hit him on top of the head and hopefully split his skull, did hit him. But it was only a glancing blow below his ear. And this seemingly harmless blow did something that Deadalus could not have planned.

Wok's head was jerked forward and to the side, a motion which would cause nothing more than a slight neckache under normal circumstances. But because of the earlier injury, the movement severed Wok's spinal cord, killing him instantly.

Deadalus whirled and swung the cable smashing into the fallen man's head before he realized that Wok was dead. He jumped over the man's crushed skull and grabbed the dropped laser gun. Crouching, Deadalus turned and faced the door. He waited.

The door remained closed. Deadalus slowly stood. The guards must not have heard anything or they would have come in instantly. Now he would have to go out to them.

Using the laser gun, Deadalus carefully melted the binding off his wrists. It was then that he realized that Wok's shot had not entirely missed him. There was a red burn about five-inches long across his hip. It wasn't bad, though it would eventually get infected and stiffen up if he didn't put some medication on it. But that would have to wait.

Deadalus checked over the laser, making sure that it was fully charged. Then he searched Wok to see if the captain carried any additional weapons, but he found none. All the time he was thinking of how to attack the two guards.

Most likely the two crew men would not be expecting him to come bursting out with a laser gun. They probably thought that if there was any trouble it would be they who came bursting in. So they most likely had taken up positions with more concern for getting in fast than in defending themselves from someone coming out. The logical setup would be for one of them to be directly across the hall from the opening door. The other would be to one side of the door.

Deadalus took a deep breath and went into action.

He burst out as the door slid open, raking his laser across the far wall. The guard who had been standing there was cut nearly in half. Deadalus, moving at full speed, ran into the torso before it had time to tumble to the floor. He used his shoulder to brace his impact against the wall, at the same time turning to look for the other guard.

The other agent crouched and fired, but his shot was hurried and went wide. Deadalus burned the man's head off.

The air in the corridor was stale with the ionized smell of the lasers. Deadalus straightened and looked quickly up and down the length of the hall, but there was no one else in sight.

Turning he went up to the nearest closed door and opened it. The cabin was empty and unused, like the one where he had been held captive. He closed the door and went to the next. This one contained personal belongings showing that it was used by one of the crew. Deadalus went in and crossed to the wardrobe. He found a uniform like the crew were wearing and put it on. It was a little loose but it would do.

He returned into the hallway and checked the two guards for additional weapons. One of them had a knife which Deadalus took and stuck in his belt. He then tossed the dead bodies into the cabin with Wok's and closed the door. He stopped for a moment, catching his breath and trying to think of where to go from here.

The only means of escape would be to get to one of the landing craft and to take off, hoping they wouldn't blast it out of space. If he was lucky and if they were confused, he might make it out quickly enough to lose them. Deadalus thought a moment longer and then hurried off in the direction of the nearest landing craft.

An emergency siren went off and the men on the bridge of the starship burst into activity.

The escaping landing craft was spotted immediately. The agent in charge signaled the craft, but got no reply. He quickly ordered two men to find out what had happened to the captain and two other men to keep track of the small craft that was weaving all over the place as if dodging for its life.

121

The two men quickly returned with word that the captain and two other crew members were dead, and the prisoner gone.

Without any confusion or hesitancy, the agent in charge turned and ordered that the escaping landing craft be destroyed.

The landing craft, dancing about on the tracking screens, was well within range of the starship's weapons. The agent manning the gun didn't even try to pinpoint the craft. He simply flooded the whole area with a wideband laser.

The resulting explosion was evident on all the viewing screens and it was out of habit that the gunner reported:

"Target destroyed, sir."

"This is Agent Felner, sir, reporting from the starship."

The voice coming over the intercom was not as confident as it could have been. The tone of the reply gave a good indication why.

"Where the hell's Wok?" Hissler's voice held death in it.

"I'm afraid, sir, that he . . . I'm sorry to report that Captain Wok is dead."

"You're going to be even sorrier when you get back to Earth. Sorry! Damndest bunch of weak-kneed agents I've ever seen! And what about Deadalus? I suppose you're sorry to report that he's out running around still, doing whatever he damn well pleases?"

"No sir. Captain Deadalus, I mean, the prisoner is dead, sir."

The speaker was silent for a moment, then Hissler's voice came back, sounding tired and disgusted.

"At least you managed to do something right. What happened?"

"Well, sir, I'm not too sure, sir. Captain Wok was down questioning the prisoner who was bound after having killed Agent Larsen."

"After what?"

"Well, sir, you see, we had just had our evening meal and Captain Wok was talking to Captain Deadalus and there were six of us there just in case, you know, as you had ordered. And, well, I don't really know why, but Captain Deadalus suspected something. He dislocated Captain Wok's neck and killed Agent Larsen before we could subdue him, sir."

"Bunch of shitheads." Hissler's muttered curse was quite audible over the intercom. "Alright Felner, continue."

"Captain Wok had just gone back down to further question the prisoner after having contacted you. As senior agent I was on the bridge at the time."

"How many agents were with Wok?"

"There were two agents outside the door, sir."

"Outside the door! What the hell were they doing *outside* the door? Why weren't they in the room?"

"I don't know, sir. Captain Wok had evidently ordered them there."

"Evidently?" Hissler's voice was so loud the intercom speaker could barely accommodate it. "Haven't you questioned them?"

"I'm afraid I couldn't. They're dead as well."

There was a long silence.

"Of course," Hissler's voice came back filled with disgust. "How silly of me not to have guessed. Tell me, Agent Felner, exactly how many agents are there left alive on the starship?"

"Ten, sir."

"That many? Please go on with your report."

"About five minutes after Captain Wok left the bridge the alarm system sounded and we noted one of our landing craft leaving the ship. I signalled it but got no reply. Two agents went down to find Captain Wok and reported back that he was dead. As senior agent in command, I ordered that the escaping landing craft be destroyed."

"And was it?"

"Yes sir."

Hissler sighed. "Alright. Try to bring the starship back to port, Felner. You're going to have to get away from the V-Two sector immediately. The place is going to be swarming with local police. They found out somehow about Deadalus's mission and are trying to make some kind of point by completing it themselves. If they catch you there, they'll destroy you and claim you were interfering. With only ten men, you're in no condition to defend yourself."

"Yes sir."

The small speaker buzzed as the connection with Earth was broken. After a moment Deadalus reached up and shut the intercom off.

He was sitting in one of the unused engineering cabins on the starship. He had gone there after setting the automatic pilot on the landing craft. He had watched as the empty landing craft had been obliterated, confirming his suspicion that to have tried to escape in it would have been too obvious. True, if he had been piloting the craft he could have possibly avoided having been so easily blasted down, but Deadalus had found it safer to never do the obvious.

At first he had been quite pleased. The odds had suddenly shifted in his favor. There were only ten left and he would certainly be able to get two or three of them by surprise before they realized that he wasn't dead. But now, having listened to the report to Hissler, he had the sinking feeling that even if he did manage to kill all of the remaining agents, it would be to no avail. He himself would survive, but he wouldn't be able to save Flo from the governor's police.

If only he could find someway to get away from the starship immediately, he might be in time to help her. But how? He had already seen what would happen to him if he tried to escape in a landing craft. If only he could disable the crew or the starship itself, just long enough to allow him to get away. They were in position now to give chase.

Deadalus sat for a few minutes, frowning in deep concentration. Then his face brightened.

Quickly he got up and, sacrificing caution for speed, made his way down to the ship's armory.

The room was a virtual warehouse of weapons, mostly for space battles. To one side were kept those used to equip the landing craft for fighting on the planetary surface. It was among these that Deadalus found what he was looking for.

They were small, egg-size, time-release bombs. Each bomb contained a biologically compounded gas, a minute whiff of which, would kill a man. Deadalus took a box of two dozen.

Using more caution than before, Deadalus hurried to the area of the ship where the landing crafts were docked. He looked around and found the nearest maintenance port off the ship's air system. He placed the carton of gas bombs inside one of the circulating ducts and set them to go off in two minutes. Then he sealed himself into one of the two remaining landing crafts and prepared for ejection. He turned on the radio that connected him with the mother ship's communication system, looked at his watch and waited.

The crew was trying to get the ship prepared to blast toward Earth, but since there were so few of them it was taking longer than usual and they were sounding a bit harried as they called back and forth to each other, checking out the different systems. And so it was nearly a minute after the bombs went off before one of the men saw the warning light.

"Trouble in the air system, sir," he radioed to the agent in charge on the bridge.

"What is it?"

"Don't know. Some kind of imbalance probably."

The air system on the starship was extremely sophisticated. It was always checking and readjusting automatically for any imbalances in the air that was passing through the ship. It also

127

had an extremely efficient filtering device that could clear the air in a very short time of any impurities. That was why Deadalus had used so much of the lethal gas. If any member of the crew could hold his breath for forty-five minutes, the air system would probably be cleared.

"Sir, the warning light's still on. There's some sort of impurity."

"Is the filtering system functioning?"

"Seems to be. Let me check. Yes sir. Oh no."

"What?"

"Seems to be some sort of gas."

There was a silence.

"My god, what'll we do?" The agent's voice sounded restricted as if he were trying to hold his breath.

"The system will clean itself." Deadalus recognized Agent Felner's voice reassuring the others.

"How did gas get in there?"

"You don't suppose that Deadalus . . ."

"Before he left?"

"Damn his bloody soul!"

Those were the last intelligible words to come over the radio. Deadalus waited another three minutes and, when the radio remained silent, decided that he had waited long enough.

He quickly plotted a course for Eurydice which, he was quite happy to see, was still nearby. The spaceship had evidently stopped as soon as it had entered free space. If he didn't run into any trouble, it would only take him two hours to get there. He knew that even that might not be soon enough to do Flo any good.

Deadalus clenched his teeth and ejected from the starship. He wasn't going to waste any time by dodging around evasively. If there was any one left alive at the controls of the starship, he was going to be an easy target.

SEVENTEEN

It only took him an hour and a half. They had souped up the landing crafts since he had last flown one.

He came in with a headlong supersonic dive, pulling up at the very last minute. He cruised at high speed at tree-top level for about a mile before he found a place he liked and set the ship down. If the tracking station at the city's transport station had been watching for him, he would have appeared on their detection screens for a total of three seconds.

Deadalus ran the two miles to the city, and then slowed down to a fast walk so as to not attract undue attention. Not wanting to risk getting lost on the unfamiliar underground trains, Deadalus stuck to the surface streets and quickly made his way to Flo's apartment.

Flo opened the door and for a moment her beautiful face looked puzzled as if she didn't recognize him. Then she threw her arms around his neck and pressed her mouth violently against his as if it had been four years and not merely four days since she had last seen him.

Deadalus indulged himself for a minute, but when the kiss started leading into other things, he broke it off.

"Flo, we've got to hurry. You've got to get out of here."

"Why? What are you talking about?"

"The police are coming. You've got to warn Whiskey and the others in your troupe. You've all got to lie low and go into hiding for awhile."

"The police? How do you know? What's going on?"

Flo stood and looked at him questioningly. She was dressed as if she was planning to go out, wearing a backless dress and thigh-high skin boots with spike heels. Deadalus could see in her eyes a flash of pride as if she had just remembered that the last time she had seen him he had left without a word.

"Flo, it's much too complicated to explain right at the moment. You're just going to have to trust me. I have it from the very best authority that Governor Washba has sent his police to kill you."

"Kill me? That's ridiculous, why would he want to kill me? I think you've made some kind of mistake."

"It's no mistake." Deadalus took hold of Flo's shoulders in his insistence to get through to her. "I can't explain it all now. Just come with me and I'll tell you the whole story later."

Flo looked at him wonderingly and then shook her head.

132

"I can't, Deadalus. I'm waiting for Whiskey. We're having a performance tonight. I don't even know who you are or what you want!" She was angry now and turned her back on him, walking away across the room. "You come here and make love to me and then leave without saying a word. Now when I've finally accepted the idea that I'm never going to see you again, you show up saying that the police have been sent to kill me and that you know all this because you're a member of the secret police. I don't believe you. I don't believe a word you're saying. You can't be a police agent."

Deadalus was just about ready to give up talking and try forcibly abducting Flo when the front door opened suddenly.

Deadalus whirled, a gun instantly in his hand, his finger on the firing button. He held back just in time. Whiskey and two other men came in. They looked like they had been running and one of them was holding his arm where it was bleeding rather profusely.

Whiskey didn't see Deadalus at first.

"Flo! Quick now, we've got to go! The police . . ." The young man stopped in midsentence when he saw Deadalus, whose gun was still pointed in their direction.

"What's he doing here?" he asked Flo through clenched teeth.

Flo moved immediately over to the injured man.

"Deadalus was trying to tell me that the police were coming here to kill us. What have you been doing, Jay? You're hurt!"

Whiskey stared long and hard at Deadalus. When he spoke it was again directed to Flo.

"Jay, Brant, and I just managed to get through before they completely encircled this place. The police are coming, Flo. But I don't see how Deadalus could have known unless he's working for them."

"Look," Deadalus said exasperated. "I know you don't trust me but at the moment you don't have any choice. We've got to get out of here fast."

Whiskey spat on the floor.

"Run! Is that all you ever think of doing? There's no way to get through, anyway. They've got this place completely encircled. And they must have about a thousand men. No. Jay, Brant, and I didn't come here to run. We came to get Flo so that we could fight and die together."

Flo came over and put her hand on the young man's arm. She was looking intently at Deadalus.

"Whiskey, Deadalus is on our side. I trust him. I think we ought to listen to what he has to say."

Whiskey shook his head. "Trust him all you want Flo. I don't."

Flo looked at Whiskey and then back at Deadalus. She let go of Whiskey's arm and walked over to stand next to Deadalus.

"Then you do what you want, Whiskey. I'm going to go with Deadalus."

Whiskey didn't move. His jaw was set as he fought with his conflicting emotions.

Deadalus walked over to him.

"I've got a ship right outside of town. It's just a short walk if we walk fast. Here, take this and follow me."

Deadalus handed his gun to Whiskey and headed for the door.

Whiskey looked at the gun in his hand in surprise.

"And just where do you plan for us to go when we get to your ship?"

Taking a handful of small contact bombs from his pocket, Deadalus turned and grinned back over his shoulder.

"Why worry about that? You said there's no way we're going to get through the circle of police."

Whiskey grinned despite himself.

EIGHTEEN

The governor's men had not known what to expect. Some of them were deployed as if expecting a riot and some were stationed as if expecting a week-long seige, but none of them were expecting what they ended up getting.

Deadalus was happy to find that, once the fighting began, Whiskey and his two friends were not only able fighters, but they were also willing to take orders and work as a team.

Getting back to the landing craft proved to be easier than anyone had suspected. As Whiskey had said, there were hundreds of policemen encircling the section of city, but exactly what they were doing was beyond Deadalus's imagination.

When they first got out on the street, an armored police vehicle approached them, ordering them to stop. Deadalus tossed a couple of bombs under it and that was the end of that. The rest of the way was a matter of being chased by a disorganized group of men who seemed to have no idea who they were chasing.

Whiskey seemed a bit disappointed when they got to the bridge leading out of the city without any more fighting.

"I don't understand why it was so easy! Do you think it's some kind of trap?"

"It would be the stupidest way to run a trap that I've ever seen," Deadalus laughed.

"How could they have so many men and let us get away like that?" Flo asked.

"They weren't really expecting any trouble. We surprised them."

"But if they weren't expecting trouble, why did they have so many men?"

"It was just a show of force. For what reason, I don't really know. I suspect it must have been political."

"Why do you say that?"

"Because," Deadalus replied, leading them across the bridge and out of the city, "anything really stupid usually turns out to be political."

One group of police spotted Deadalus and his companions as they crossed the bridge and almost managed to catch them. Deadalus, almost leisurely, blew up a span of the bridge, bringing the pursuers to a complete halt. They went the rest of the way to the landing craft unbothered.

The spaceship was exactly as Deadalus had left it and they hurried aboard gratefully. Deadalus showed Flo where the medical supplies were so that she could fix Jay's injured arm and then he instructed Whiskey how to use the ship's laser. It was a fairly simple skill and Whiskey caught on right away. Deadalus then

138

ordered them all to strap in as he sat in the pilot's chair and prepared to blast off.

He had no real plans of what he was going to do at this point. Deadalus just thought that if they could get away, out of the V-Two sector, they would be alright. They'd just go to the next sector with a suitable planet, and when they got there Deadalus would figure out a way to get them down undetected and into a city.

Before blasting off Eurydice though, he automatically monitored the radio to see if there was any traffic in the nearby area. Much to his surprise, he found that the entire area was flooded with the governor's police crafts. Perplexed, he listened for a couple of minutes and finally was able to make out that they were searching for Wok's starship.

There was no way they could take off without being observed. They weren't going to be able to defend themselves against all the spacecraft that was in the area, not with the untrained crew that he had.

"Here come the police," Whiskey called. "Boy, they're just sitting ducks from here. I'm going to blast them."

"No." Deadalus's command was firm and absolute.

"What do you mean? I've got them right here in sight."

"You fire that laser without my direct order and I'm going to throw you off this ship."

Whiskey stared at Deadalus in surprise and anger. He opened his mouth to say something, but then thought better of it.

"Do you mind telling me why not?" the young man asked finally.

"Because there's nothing they can do to us now. You don't go around just killing people."

"But they were trying to kill us!"

"That was their job. They can't hurt us now, so there's no reason to hurt them."

"They're over on this side, too," Brant called. "They'll be close enough to shoot us in a minute."

"Alright. Does anyone know where the governor's detention camp is?"

The artists looked at each other in wonder.

"It's at the foot of the Nepal hills," Jay replied.

"Is it hard to find?"

"No, you can't miss it. It's just west of the city."

Deadalus took off, flying so low over the heads of the astonished police that the jets singed the hair on the tallest of them.

"What do you want with the detention camp?" Whiskey asked after he had regained his breath, which he had lost suddenly during the takeoff.

"I just thought that since you wanted to get some practice shooting in, I'd give you something to shoot at. Now I'm going to make two passes over it and I want you to knock out any towers and perimetric defenses they have. Then we'll land as close as we can, and Brant and I will go in and do some liberating. Whiskey, you stay on the port side gun. Jay, you take the other. Alright?"

There was a tense silence as the artists struggled to accept the job being given to them. Finally, the strongest of them spoke up. It was Flo.

"What do we do if you don't come back? None of us know how to fly this thing."

"Don't worry, I'll be back. I'm not planning to stay in this place. I've heard terrible reports about their room service."

There was a moment of silence and then Deadalus added:

"But whatever you do, Flo, please don't let them take you alive."

NINETEEN

The detention camp was hard to miss. Built right into the side of the mountain, its construction was as crude as its intended purpose.

As they approached it at medium speed, Deadalus was able to make out the main structures. There was one barracks-type building that jutted out from the mountainside and led back into the rock earth. In a half circle around this structure was an electronic fence, which was a low-power laser relayed between a series of poles. The large generator needed to maintain the fence was located outside of it, set back against the hills. The only other visible structures were the two guard towers topped with lights and weapons.

Deadalus climbed in preparation of diving.

"Alright, everybody hold on," he called out cheerfully. "I'll take the generator out, you two on the guns, try to get the towers."

Deadalus dropped the nose of the spacecraft in what was almost a ninety-degree dive. He waited until they were quite low before firing

143

two rockets at the generator. He heard both lasers being fired and waited till the last possible moment to pull out of the dive.

The G-force on the turn was more than Deadalus had expected.

"Everyone alright?" he called out. "I'll try to be less rough on the next one."

As he turned around above the detention camp, Deadalus saw that one of the towers and the generator had been knocked out.

There had been no return fire whatsoever. The weapons in the towers were designed for being used against people trying to break out, not spacecrafts from the outside trying to break in. Even if Deadalus hadn't taken the guards totally by surprise, there would have been very little that they could have done to stop the attack.

On the second dive, Deadalus let the lasers take out the other tower while he dropped a missile in front of the building built out of the mountain, crumbling the front facade.

Deadalus pulled out of the dive, watching a dozen uniformed guards scrambled for cover on the ground behind them. There still hadn't been any return fire, and there wouldn't be until the prison called in some air support. Deadalus figured that they would probably have about ten minutes before the first spacecraft could come to the rescue of the prison. They'd have to work fast.

"Alright, nice shooting, you guys. I'm taking her down. You ready, Brant?"

Deadalus landed the ship inside the electronic fence. Now there was some light firing from a few guards behind the rubble of one of the towers as well as from the fallen front of the main building.

Whiskey trained the ship's gun on those in the building, giving Deadalus and Brant cover as they jumped out of the ship and ran to shelter behind some of the fallen facade. This protected them from those who were in the building, but Deadalus found that they were exposed to the guards who were behind the fallen guard tower.

Deadalus and Brant dove to the ground as the guards fired at them. They returned the fire but it was clear that they were going to be pinned down for awhile.

"Brant, we don't have time for this," Deadalus said.

Brant looked at him for a moment.

"Fine with me, Captain. You want to tell them guys or should I?"

Deadalus grinned. Brant's slow drawl had been unhurried, as if completely unaffected by the rapid fire all around them.

"I'm going to toss some timed explosives into the building. Trouble is, I have no idea where the guards are. So what we're going to have to do is follow the explosives in, hoping that the guards will keep their heads down long enough for us to find cover. Pretty risky, I know. But if we wait around here, they'll have a whole star fleet on top of us."

Deadalus set the explosives and tossed them. He counted to three under his breath.

"Let's go!"

He leaped to his feet just as the explosives went off and for a moment Deadalus could feel himself being pushed back by the shockwaves. Then his feet were pumping, leaping over rubble, with Brant right behind him.

Deadalus had no idea where the guards were, but he was certain of one place that they weren't. He ran directly for the spot of rubble where his explosives had landed. Deadalus dove headfirst into the dirt. When there was no firing, he raised his head and looked around.

His explosives had been a lucky shot. The remains of three guards lay scattered about. Nearby were another two guards, either dead or knocked out from the concussion.

Brant tapped him on the shoulder and pointed down the hallway that seemed to lead back into the mountain. Two guards, carrying a wounded comrade between them, were hurrying away. When Deadalus fired on them, the two guards dropped their friend, wildly returned the fire, and then ran out of sight farther into the building, leaving the wounded guard.

Deadalus leaped to his feet and rushed toward the wounded man. He no longer bothered to worry about telling Brant what to do. The young man seemed adept and followed Deadalus's lead automatically. With weapons ready, they approached the guard.

When they got to him, Deadalus could see that the guard didn't have a gun, which didn't really matter, because the guard didn't have

146

any hands to shoot a gun with anyway. One entire arm and half of the other had been ripped away. Emergency tourniquets had been put on to stop the bleeding and a strong tranquilizer had evidently been administered, for the guard was lying on the ground mumbling incoherently when Deadalus and Brant got to him.

Deadalus looked in the direction where the two other guards had fled, then reached down and picked the fallen guard up by his shirt collar.

"Where are the prisoners?" Deadalus shook the man. The guard stopped mumbling and looked at Deadalus blankly.

"Which way to the prisoners, damn you!"

Deadalus shook him again and the man began to whimper. The guard was too far gone to understand his question. Deadalus holstered his gun and took out his knife. With one quick motion he slit the man's trembling lower lip.

The guard cried with pain as the blood spurted out and he moved as if to reach up to his face. But he had no hands to reach with and the motion stopped in mid-air.

"Where are the prisoners?" Deadalus demanded.

This time the half-dead man understood them and quickly indicated a passageway that led to the right, back into the mountain. Deadalus dropped the man and he and Brant ran quickly down the passage indicated.

The passage led down and after a little way made a sharp turn. Deadalus looked around the corner and saw three guards standing together talking excitedly, not really sure what was going on. Deadalus took out an explosive, set it for three seconds, then rolled it around the corner toward the group. The ensuing blast echoed loudly through the underground hall. Deadalus and Brant sprinted through the smoke-filled corridor to where the three guards were lying.

They had been knocked down and were somewhat stunned by the blast, but unhurt. Before they could get to their feet and regain their dropped weapons, Deadalus and Brant were on top of them. The three men wisely gave up and raised their hands in surrender.

"Where are the prisoners?" Deadalus demanded as Brant gathered up their guns.

One of the men indicated a door right next to them. The door had a small viewing screen and Deadalus activated it and looked in.

The room on the other side was not very large and the fifty or so men who were in it were crowded together, lying or squatting on the bare floor.

"Open it up," Deadalus ordered, turning his gun on the guards.

After a brief hesitation, one of them stepped forward and put a key in the palm lock and the door slid open.

The smell was horrible, but the looks on the faces of the prisoners that turned toward them was even worse. Most of them looked either half dead or half crazy. All of them showed signs of having been tortured.

Deadalus ushered the guards inside at gunpoint and then stepped in after them. There was a stirring among the prisoners as they saw the guards with their hands raised, and those that could get to their feet did so, crowding closer. One of the prisoners pushed his way forward with an air of authority.

"What's going on?" he asked Deadalus.

"I'm setting you free."

There was a murmur among the crowd and they surged forward only to be stopped by the prisoner who had assumed control.

"Who are you and why do you want to set us free?" the man asked suspiciously.

"My name is Captain Deadalus. I'm a political outlaw, just as you are. In return for setting you free I want some of you to help me. I need enough men to crew a starship. It's a wild gamble and our chances of surviving are very slim. And if we do make it, those who come with me are going to have to be willing to give up Eurydice, because we're not coming back. But on the other hand, those who stay here don't have much of a future either. I'm sure you know that. The fence and the towers are down, but there are still a lot of armed guards about. If you do manage to get away, you're going to be running from the police for the rest of your lives."

"How many men do you need?" the lead prisoner asked.

"I need at least ten, though I would be happy for more."

"Well, I'm one for you," the prisoner replied, then he turned to the crowd of prisoners behind him. "All those who are for going with me and the captain here, over to this side, you others over there."

Twenty men in all volunteered to go with Deadalus. As he looked over them, Deadalus realized that they were in such bad condition that he'd be lucky to find ten ablebodied among them. Deadalus passed out the guards' guns among the remaining prisoners, giving up his own as well.

It was then that the prisoners really understood that they were in control and could fight back. With a sudden sound of rage, about twelve men jumped on the three prison guards and started beating them to death.

Deadalus turned from the disgusting sight.

"Can't you stop them?" he asked the leader who had joined with him.

The prisoner was watching the bloody scene with a small grin.

"Not without shooting them, Captain. They've been treated too badly to be denied revenge."

There was the sound of an explosion outside.

"Alright, let's get out of here!" Deadalus shouted. "Brant, you take the front. You men stay in a line as close together as you can. Everyone who can is to help anyone who can't move as well. I'll bring up the rear."

Despite the number of injured men, they moved quickly. The feeling of urgency made the prisoners push themselves faster. There were the sounds of more explosions outside and Deadalus was able to make out the whizzing sound of a spacecraft. The police cruisers had gotten there faster than he had hoped for. With Deadalus's urging, the line of men moved faster.

When they finally broke out into the open, Deadalus could see that there were two police cruisers attacking his spacecraft. Whiskey was doing a good job of keeping them at bay, but even the most experienced gunner wouldn't have been able to last very long, stuck on the ground fighting against two ships.

One of the cruisers fired at the line of men who were running toward the spacecraft. A number of the men fell, and as Deadalus stopped to help one of them, he saw Flo jump out of the ship and begin helping the other prisoners in.

The man Deadalus was helping was unconscious and he threw him over his shoulders. He ran with him to the ship, where he handed him over to Brant. Then he hurried to the pilot's chair.

"Everybody hold on!" he called. "Whiskey, keep your finger on that laser button."

They blasted off at full throttle in front of one of the diving police cruisers. Whiskey's laser, which he was holding as Deadalus had said, swept across the front of the cruiser before it had time to react to the blasting off spacecraft. There was an explosion as the laser swept across it and then a few moments later a much larger explosion as the cruiser crashed into the mountain.

The second cruiser had just completed its turn in preparation for another dive. It fired at

Deadalus's ship, but Deadalus maneuvered out of the way. The cruisers were faster and bigger and Deadalus knew that he couldn't outrun them. His ship was more maneuverable and its weapons were better designed for this sort of battle than the police's were.

Deadalus acted as if he was trying to run. He headed away from the oncoming cruiser, but not at full speed. He concentrated on dodging the other's missiles while the cruiser gained on them. Deadalus waited until the cruiser had picked top speed and then he pulled back and over in a loop. The police cruiser was going too fast to follow the tight maneuver and overshot them. When Deadalus leveled out from the loop, he was directly behind the police spacecraft.

Deadalus fired two missiles, both direct hits. Then he pulled up and away from the flying wreckage of the demolished cruiser. Now all he had to do was weave his way through a couple dozen more police cruisers and take over the Empirical starship. All he had for crew was a bunch of half-dead and desperate outlaws who probably didn't know the first thing about manning a starship in battle.

Deadalus grinned. Nothing to it. All they needed was a little bit of luck. And a few miracles.

TWENTY

Five minutes later their little bit of luck ran out.

They were spotted by a police cruiser. Deadalus knocked it out but not before the ship radioed their position. Two more ships closed in, lasers on full blast.

"Hold on tight!" Deadalus called. "Whiskey, Brant, get on those side guns. We've got ourselves a fight."

Deadalus dove at full speed then slammed to a standstill, grinning as two missiles passed a few yards in front of the ship's nose. Then he looped back under, once again at full throttle. One of the police ships was caught completely by surprise by Deadalus's maneuver, Deadalus blasted it.

Twisting away from the wreckage Deadalus searched for the other cruiser. A sudden, teeth-grinding lurch told him where it was. It was right on his tail. And the ship had been hit.

Cursing, Deadalus fired both rear missiles without looking and tried to loop back over. The ship shuddered violently as Deadalus gave it the throttle and suddenly careened sideways instead of looping. One of the thrusting jets had been knocked out.

Deadalus had the police ship on the screen now and he saw it diving to maneuver out of the way of the missiles he'd fired. The pilot of the other ship was good. He had even been expecting Deadalus's attempt to loop and had twisted back away where he'd have a clean shot at Deadalus's ship. The maneuver that Deadalus ended up with surprised the other pilot as much as it did Deadalus.

The thrusting jet which had gone out, causing the ship to dive sideways, suddenly came on again, throwing them into a spin. Deadalus pulled out of it and ended up next to the police cruiser.

Before he had time to give the order, Deadalus heard the port side laser fire and saw the beam rake across the side of the enemy's ship. He heard Whiskey give a whoop of delight as the police ship exploded.

"I got him!"

"Sure did, Whiskey, nice shooting."

Deadalus felt the controls go stiff. He tested them and they responded, but very sluggishly. They weren't going to be able to outmaneuver anyone now. Not only that, it seemed likely that the thrusters would go out altogether, leaving them stranded.

"I smell something burning," Brant called out.

Deadalus smelled it, too. His brows knit together for a minute. Then he turned and quickly punched in some questions on the com-

154

puter. He studied the display for a moment. Turning back to the controls he set a course and then gently accelerated. At three-quarters throttle the ship started vibrating violently, so he slacked off until they were fairly smooth and then locked it in place.

"What's going on, Captain?" one of the men asked.

Deadalus turned and looked over the group of people strapped behind him. They were pale but otherwise alright.

"Our ship has been disabled. I'm going to see if I can get us to Kraton."

"What are we going to do on Kraton?"

"Check the damage to the ship and see if it's repairable, look over our alternatives if it isn't."

There was a silence as they thought about what he was saying.

"Sounds like a holiday compared to where I've been," one of the former prisoners joked.

Deadalus grinned with relief. They were a good bunch of men. They weren't complaining or arguing, and that was going to make it that much easier. He was going to have enough to worry about without that.

He turned back to the controls, scanning the radar and communication waves. They were heading away from the bulk of searching police cruisers. Hopefully they wouldn't pick up their trail for a while. It was going to take them fifteen minutes at this speed to reach Kraton. Deadalus knew that to reach the small planet completely unnoticed would be asking too much. He just hoped that they'd have a strong headstart by the time they were located so that they could reach the planet without being caught.

Deadalus scanned the monitors for a few minutes and when he was sure that they weren't being followed he unstrapped himself and got up. He walked to the back of the craft and looked in the engine room. He couldn't see where the damage was, but he could smell some wires smoldering. He sealed off the compartment and then drained the air out of it, which would guarantee against any fires.

Deadalus was looking through the food storage compartment when Flo came up next to him.

"How bad does it look?" she asked in a low voice.

Deadalus shrugged.

"Our chances never did look good, Flo. They're a little less now. That's all."

Flo watched him wide-eyed.

"Is there anything I can do to help?" she asked.

Deadalus found what he was looking for and stood up smiling at her.

"Yeah, you can pass this around," he said, handing her a large plastic jug.

Flo looked at the label.

"Rum?"

"It's not really," Deadalus whispered. "But it will do the trick. It's some artificially manufactured stuff. Tastes awful, but I don't think most of these men are going to notice that. You can let the wounded men have as much as they want, but I don't want any of the ablebodied men to get drunk. Alright?"

Flo smiled at him and nodded.

As Deadalus looked into her eyes, he wanted to take her in his arms and somehow call a halt to this whole stupid game. He just wanted to take her away from all this where they could be alone.

But it wasn't a game. They were playing for keeps and there was no way to stop it until one side lost.

Deadalus kissed Flo gently on the top of her head and went back to the pilot's seat and strapped himself in. He checked the controls. They were seven minutes from Kraton. He watched the radar detection light which would indicate the first warning if they were spotted.

As the rum was passed around, a few conversations started and Deadalus could feel the pent-up tension easing from the men. Deadalus looked at the time, trying to calculate how long it had been since he had woken up on the starship. After a minute he gave up. All he knew was that his lack of sleep was catching up with him.

They were close enough now for Deadalus to get a visual on Kraton. It certainly didn't look like the kind of place that he would choose to spend a holiday. It was entirely composed of mountains and rugged, dry cliffs cut jaggedly across by deep chasms. Formidable, and if he could get the ship down alright it would be a perfect place to hide.

The radar picked up a ship back where

Deadalus had had the battle with the two cruisers. Deadalus sighed. A few minutes more and they would have been home free. The radar screen showed the other ship suddenly accelerating toward them, indicating that the police cruiser had spotted them on their radar.

Deadalus checked his coordinates. It wouldn't matter too much. The police ship was too far away to be able to get a visual on them before they landed. And once Deadalus got their ship down in those mountains, the enemy's radar wasn't going to do them any good.

Deadalus flipped the switch to take the ship out of automatic control and put it back into manual.

Nothing happened.

He tested the controls. The ship wouldn't respond. He flipped the switch repeatedly but it was no good. The ship was stuck in automatic drive, following the directions that he had plotted on the computer.

The ship was taking them to Kraton alright. The only problem was that Deadalus always plotted to the center of the planet to compensate for any marginal errors. And so that was exactly where the ship was going to try to take them.

The screen showed fifty-eight seconds to impact.

▉▉▉▉▉▉▉▉▉▉▉▉▉▉▉▉▉▉▉▉▉▉▉▉▉▉▉ TWENTY-ONE

Deadalus pushed again on the controls, trying to slow them down from their headlong plunge toward the planet. The ship still didn't respond.

Thinking quickly, Deadalus turned to the computer, and as fast as he could, he punched in a program telling it to cut the throttle jets.

The ship responded. The throttle jets were turned off, but they were still falling much too quickly. Deadalus could sense the ship heating up as they hit the planet's atmosphere. He still didn't have any control over the ship. Working incredibly quickly he programmed the computer for full reverse thrusters. But he knew that it was too late. They were going to crash.

They slammed into the ground, bouncing once, and then ground to a stop. Deadalus had the computer cut the engines. Sudden silence filled the ship as Deadalus turned and looked at the men behind him.

"I take it we're there, Captain," Brant drawled.

"Apparently so," Deadalus replied, unstrapping and getting up. "Is everyone alright?"

"There's a man out over here," someone called.

Deadalus went over and found that one of the men from the detention camp had lost consciousness. He got the medical supplies and brought him to. Then he put Flo and Whiskey in charge of the food and medical supplies and took Brant out with him to look over the damage.

The ship was resting between two high, rocky hills. Deadalus was gratified to see that they would be difficult to spot from the air. Dusk was settling, making it nearly impossible for anyone to find them, if they had been seen coming down.

"How long does night last here?" he asked Brant as he looked over the damaged nose of the ship.

"Six hours. This time of year daylight is ten hours. How does the ship look?"

"Not very good. You know anything about fixing spaceships, Brant?"

"Not me. If you need something fixed, Whiskey's the one to ask. That man can fix anything that's fixable and even some things that aren't."

The front of the ship was bent and crumpled, but the hull was still in one piece. The reverse thrusters must have helped more than he hoped. Then too, the gravity on Kraton was less than on Earth. The hull looked like it would hold if he could get the ship back in operation, but that was a big if.

They went back and joined the others to eat.

160

Deadalus hated to waste the night, which was their best cover for doing anything, but he didn't see what they could do. Despite Brant's declarations of Whiskey's ability, Deadalus seriously doubted that they were going to get the ship flying again. The landing craft was such a complex piece of machinery that it usually took extensive knowledge and specialized tools.

Deadalus finished his rations and went outside to think over the options. If they couldn't repair the ship, their best bet would be to hide it and take some supplies up into the hills. Deadalus had noticed a number of caves. That was what they should be doing now and not take the risk of being spotted during the daylight. The men from the detention camp were in very poor condition and everyone needed rest, including himself.

Deadalus was in top shape and could go for a long period of time on very little rest, but he couldn't go indefinitely.

The best idea was for them to get a good six hours sleep. They could look the ship over in the morning. If they couldn't repair it, they could camouflage it and hope they weren't spotted in the ten hours of daylight. The next night they could move into the hills.

Deadalus walked up a small nearby hill to look over the area in the last fading light. Kraton was as desolate closeup as it had appeared to be from space. It was rough, hard stone. There didn't even seem to be any dirt, just rock. The atmosphere must have been a recent addition because half of the features were craters, and there was no vegetation whatsoever on this part of the planet.

Darkness fell and Deadalus looked at the myriad of stars spread like a handful of dusty jewels against a velvet cushion. Nowhere was there a familiar constellation.

Deadalus heard someone come out of the landing craft and he turned to see Flo coming up the hill behind him, a blanket wrapped around her to keep out the chill that was creeping into the night air.

Deadalus watched her dark silhouette as she climbed the hill and he could feel the image burning into his memory, never to be forgotten. She smiled as she came up to him.

"Everyone's fallen asleep, Deadalus. Aren't you going to come in and get some rest?"

"I was just about to." He put his arms around her.

She looked up at him, studying his face.

"I don't understand you, Deadalus. I wish I knew what you're thinking."

"I'm thinking, dear lady, that I would like very much to kiss you."

Flo put her arms around his neck as he pressed his mouth against hers.

The kiss, which started gently, quickly turned passionate. Flo pulled away and buried her face on Deadalus's shoulder.

"I don't know what it is, Deadalus. Every time you touch me I get all shaky and all I can think about is making love to you."

Deadalus laughed. "What's wrong with that?"

162

Flo looked up at him.

"Nothing's wrong with it. It's just that it comes at inappropriate times. Like earlier when we were in space and you asked me to pass the rum around, what I really wanted to do was drag you into some storage compartment and have sex."

"Damn lucky I didn't know that. We would have really been in trouble."

"I'm not joking, Deadalus."

"Neither am I," he replied and then kissed her, this time not even starting gently.

Flo returned his kiss passionately. She pressed her body hard against him and he could feel her firm breasts rubbing against his chest. He ran his hand down the curve of her back to the back of her thigh. She bit down on his lip, almost in agony, and he could feel her knees trembling as if about to give way.

Deadalus picked her up in his arms and laid her gently down on the hard ground of Kraton.

TWENTY-TWO

Flo was sitting, shaking his shoulder.

"Deadalus, come on, wake up!" Her voice was an urgent whisper.

Deadalus's tired body fought for sleep.

"Deadalus, please. There's something out here."

His senses became fully alert. He sat up looking around.

Everything was dark and still. He could just make out the shapes of the rocks around them and the silhouette of the landing craft at the bottom of the hill.

There was no sound, no movement. But Deadalus's skin tingled. There was something out here. His nose picked up a faint odor, somehow familiar. Recognition tried to work its way from the back of his mind. There was something important that he had forgotten, something which he needed to remember.

Silently, Deadalus put his hand on Flo's shoulder. They had to get back to the ship. He stood up slowly and then bent over to help Flo to her feet.

There was a hiss.

Deadalus whirled, knife instantly in hand. But it was too late.

There were claws in his shoulder and teeth at his throat, grabbing for his jugular. Then there were more claws and teeth scratching and biting at his legs.

Deadalus slashed and stabbed. He knocked one off his back. Instantly another was on his other shoulder. He lost his footing, falling heavily to the ground.

He could smell the hot animal breath. His hands grew slippery with blood. He kicked, rolled, punched, and slashed, but they still kept coming. Teeth and claws, biting and scratching. He couldn't keep them off.

Then Flo did something Deadalus hadn't thought of. She screamed.

The ship's lights came on, flooding the hill in a brilliant white light. The pack of animals scattered, dodging back into the shadows.

Deadalus picked himself up, looking at the two animals he'd killed. He recognized them now from his background reading on Eurydice. They were gatos, the genetically engineered cats brought here to help with mining.

Fortunately they were small, the size of housecats. If they had been any bigger Deadalus wouldn't have had a chance against them.

He helped Flo up. She was unhurt, but Deadalus could feel her knees trembling from fright.

"It's alright now, Flo. It's OK."

She tried bravely to smile.

"At least I didn't wake up alone this time," she said, trying to joke. Her voice cracked and she started crying.

Deadalus held her tight and by the time Whiskey and Brant got up the hill, guns ready, Flo was once again composed.

Back in the ship Deadalus cleaned his wounds, pouring on liberal doses of disinfectant. Though the cuts themselves were fairly superficial, there was a great risk of them becoming infected.

As much as the medicine stung, Deadalus felt he deserved it. Falling asleep out there was inexcusable. He was lucky they weren't dead.

Deadalus didn't like the way things were going. They were in a bad position without adding to it by their own mistakes.

He went over to Whiskey, who was sitting with Flo, talking in a low voice.

"Whiskey, Brant says you're good at fixing things."

Whiskey stared at him without replying.

"Care to come give me a hand, see if we can fix the ship?"

Whiskey kept staring at him almost belligerently. For a moment Deadalus thought he was going to say no. But then the young man got to his feet and followed Deadalus back into the engine compartment.

Deadalus explained the nature of the problem while he ran through some circuit checks. Whiskey still hadn't said anything and Deadalus was beginning to think that the young poet wasn't going to be any help.

Whiskey gave a low whistle of surprise.

Deadalus looked back over his shoulder. Whiskey was looking through the manual of engine schematics.

"Where the hell did you get this ship anyway!" he finally burst out, looking at Deadalus suspiciously.

"Why?"

Whiskey pointed to something on the schematic.

"This circuit interloop here with the computer, and over here, this power over-riding switch, I've never seen anything so sophisticated. Why, half of these computer interfacings are still on the drawing boards where I come from. How'd you get a ship like this?"

Deadalus hesitated. He hadn't told anyone yet that he was an ex-member of the Empirical secret police. But if he expected Whiskey to be willing to work with him he was going to have to be open with the young man. Deadalus knew he'd have to tell Whiskey, but he had hoped he could put it off until later. He had a good idea what everyone's reaction was going to be.

"The ship belongs to the Empirical secret police," he said finally.

"And just what the hell are you doing with a Secret Police ship, Captain?"

"Until a few days ago I was an agent for them."

Whiskey tensed. Deadalus glanced at the young man's side and saw that he still had a hand gun holstered on his hip. Deadalus turned back to the circuits he was testing.

"Never heard of anyone defecting from the secret police," Whiskey growled.

Deadalus didn't reply.

"I'm afraid I don't trust you, Deadalus. Your story sounds suspicious."

Deadalus turned around. Whiskey had the gun trained on him.

"Damn it, Whiskey, haven't I been fighting right beside you? Who was it that got you away from the governor's police? Whose idea was it to go to the detention camp?"

"Sure, you've been fighting the governor's men real good. That doesn't surprise me. Doesn't mean you aren't still working for the Empirical police. This looks like a setup to me. What were you doing on Eurydice in the first place?"

Deadalus looked at him steadily.

"I was sent to kill you and Flo."

Whiskey reacted with expectable surprise.

Deadalus explained the story of how Whiskey and Flo had been ordered to be killed to teach Governor Washba a lesson, and how the governor found out and was trying to save face by getting to the artists first.

"You mean you were going to kill us because that fat-assed governor hasn't been behaving?"

"That was what I was sent to do."

"And why should I believe that that isn't exactly what you still intend to do?"

"Because I've had a dozen easy chances to do just that! If I wanted to kill you, you would have been dead long ago."

He saw a sudden change come over Whiskey's face as the young man recognized the truth of what Deadalus was saying. Whiskey knew that Deadalus could have easily killed him that night at Flo's apartment and wouldn't have needed an excuse.

Deadalus turned back to what he'd been doing.

"Excuse me, Captain," Whiskey said, the tone of his voice showing a new respect. "But I think the problem's in this circuit over here."

Whiskey, it turned out, was quite adept at fixing things. As he worked on the ship he explained that he had been trained as a top design engineer. Because of his political activism and because all the jobs in that field involved working for the government, he had never been able to get employment.

"Does it look repairable?" Deadalus asked after Whiskey had fully analyzed the problem.

"I'm pretty sure I can fix it. I'll have to work on the thruster jet from the outside though."

"How long do you think it'll take?"

"Hard to say. Couple of hours maybe."

The more he thought about it, the less Deadalus liked their position. It would be light in an hour or so. If the police cruiser had been tracking them, they'd know that Deadalus's ship had landed on Kraton. If they put on a full-scale search it would only be a matter of time before they were spotted. The only thing in Deadalus's favor was that the police didn't know that his ship was disabled. Because of that they'd use more caution while searching. That would slow them down.

Deadalus chewed his lip and waited. There was nothing else he could do but wait to see if Whiskey could complete the repairs in time. He hoped the repairs would hold long enough for them to fight their way back to the starship, and that the governor's men didn't get to the ship before them.

Deadalus didn't like having his fate in the hands of chance, but he couldn't really complain. He'd already gotten much farther than he thought he would. The odds against them were so overwhelming that there was no chance of getting free. It was a matter of how long they could go before getting caught.

Whiskey sent Deadalus back to the front to run through some control tests. In the viewing screen Deadalus saw that the sky was starting to lighten. On the communication bands he heard a number of ships close by, though he couldn't tell where.

"Looks all set in here," Whiskey called over the intercom. "I'll have to go outside to work on the thruster jet."

Deadalus went outside with Whiskey and helped him climb into the jet. He heard the young man muttering curses as he looked over the damage.

"I don't know," Whiskey called after awhile.

"What's the matter?"

Whiskey gave him a technical description that completely lost him.

"What does that mean? Is it fixable?"

"No. But I might be able to work around it. What I need is a metal rod about a foot long."

Deadalus went back into the ship. He looked through the tools and spare parts but couldn't see anything suitable. He looked for something to salvage and settled for the hinge on the food cupboard. He took the hinge outside and using a laser gun, cut off a foot-length. He handed it to Whiskey.

"Yeah, that should work."

A couple of minutes later Flo came out.

"Deadalus? Brant says he sees a police cruiser."

Deadalus hurried inside, leaving Flo to help Whiskey. Sure enough the screen showed a cruiser five miles away, searching back and forth. Deadalus watched it make a couple of passes. At the rate it was going it would take twenty minutes for it to be overhead. When it got there Deadalus would have a choice. He could sit still and hope that by some impossible chance the cruiser wouldn't spot them, or he could fire at it and hope that his first shot would knock it out. It was unlikely that he'd get a second one.

Five minutes passed. Deadalus told Brant to make sure everyone was awake and ready for whatever happened. Another three minutes passed. Deadalus checked the screen and saw another cruiser on the far horizon. He cursed under his breath.

"Someone get Whiskey back in here on the double."

Five more minutes passed. Deadalus tracked the approaching ship, ready to fire the missiles at the first sign that the cruiser had spotted them.

"Whiskey, Brant, get on the side lasers. Keep your eyes open."

"Whiskey's still outside," Brant replied.

"Damn it! Didn't someone go out and get him?"

"I think Flo did."

Deadalus had a sudden sinking sensation, but there was no time for him to think about it. The cruiser, which had been moving at a steady pace, hesitated slightly. Deadalus's trained eye picked up the slight difference in movement, recognizing instantly what it meant.

Both ships fired at the same time. The cruiser's shot went wide, but just barely, shaking the ship with the closeness of its blast. Deadalus's shot went true and the police cruiser exploded into a bright orange ball of fire.

Deadalus ran over to the exit port to call Whiskey in. He saw Flo lying motionless on the ground. Whiskey was next to her, struggling to his feet.

Something inside of Deadalus went cold. He ran down and picked up Flo, as Whiskey stood up looking around in a daze.

"I fixed it," he muttered.

"Run, damn it, run!" Deadalus yelled as Whiskey stood dazed and staring at the second police cruiser bearing down at them.

Brant fired the starboard laser just as the

cruiser started to dive. The cruiser fired but missed as it maneuvered to dodge Brant's shot.

Deadalus ran back in the ship with Flo and Whiskey following him. Deadalus handed the still unconscious Flo to someone and then ran to strap himself into the pilot's seat.

"Is it going to work, Whiskey?"

"I think so. It should work even better than before," the young man replied, still unsteady.

Deadalus fired two quick volleys at the police cruiser which had turned around and was readying for another dive.

"Everyone strap in," Deadalus called while tracking the enemy ship.

Fortunately, the pilot of the other ship wasn't too adept. It appeared that he was going to hold back and circle. Probably waiting for reinforcements.

Deadalus switched on the controls, running quickly through the preflight tests, watching the indicators carefully for any sign of aberrant behavior. Everything looked normal.

He glanced over his shoulder to make sure everyone was strapped in. Brant was at the starboard gun. Someone had taken Whiskey's spot at the port gun. Deadalus glanced at Flo, who was still unconscious, and forced himself to look away.

He blasted off at full throttle.

The acceleration was so great it nearly caught Deadalus off guard. Not only had Whiskey fixed the thrusters but he had improved them.

The pilot of the police cruiser was caught completely off guard. Panicked that he might lose Deadalus's ship, the pilot made a fatal mistake, a completely predictable maneuver.

Deadalus saw that the enemy pilot was putting his ship into a turn, obviously in order to take off directly after them. Deadalus put his ship into a 180-degree flip, so when the cruiser pilot completed his turn he found Deadalus's ship coming straight down his throat at full speed.

Deadalus fired a missile and immediately twisted away to dodge any possible return fire. But the enemy pilot had been too surprised even for that.

Deadalus's missile found its mark and the pilot of the police cruiser never got a chance to repent for his mistake.

TWENTY-FOUR

The return trip to the starship went smoothly. Deadalus's concentration was fully occupied with dodging and maneuvering around the enemy ships, and he had no time to worry about anything else. At the last moment, three cruisers started to close in and would have caught them had they not been so close to the starship.

Once Deadalus got aboard the starship, the police cruisers didn't have a chance. Without plotting a course or checking the ship, Deadalus shot the starship dancing light-years out into free space. After half an hour of wild unplotted jumping, they were completely lost. It would take two days for Deadalus to trace back and find where they were, but now that they were out of reach of the governor's men, there was plenty of time.

Deadalus put the ship in stationary and went to take care of his new crew.

He organized those who were ablebodied to help get food and clothes and to tend to the wounded. He got two men to help collect and

177

toss the bodies of Wok and the other secret police agents out into space. Then finally, he went to see Flo.

She was in one of the cabins, knocked out by a heavy tranquilizer, her face freshly bandaged. Whiskey was sitting next to her bed.

"How's she doing?" Deadalus asked in a low voice.

Whiskey shook his head and got up and left the room.

Deadalus watched him leave and then sat down in the chair next to the bed.

He sat looking at her bandaged face. The activities of the past few days caught up with him at once. He suddenly realized how tired he was, every muscle and bone in his body ached with fatigue. He dozed off.

A soft moan woke him. Flo's eyes opened and there was a painful, frightened look in them. Her lips were trying to form some word and Deadalus leaned closer.

"Flo? It's alright, just take it easy."

"It's not alright," she said, her voice nothing more than a hoarse whisper.

Deadalus grasped her hand in his, not knowing what to say. Flo closed her eyes for a moment in obvious pain and then opened them again. She managed a small smile.

"Did we win?" she whispered.

Deadalus nodded, unable to speak. He picked her up and held her in his arms.

"I guess you're going to have to take care of Whiskey and all the rest for me," she whispered.

"Don't leave me, Flo, don't leave me."

Deadalus held her tighter as if by sheer strength he was going to keep her alive.

She leaned her head against his shoulder. She was dead.

Two hours later, Captain Deadalus emerged from the cabin and gave orders to Brant to gather everyone who wasn't confined to a bed into the mess room.

Fifteen minutes later Brant came to report that they were all assembled.

"Only I couldn't find Whiskey anywhere."

"Couldn't find him? This is a starship, Brant. We're in the middle of space. He couldn't have just gone out for a drink."

"I know. I looked everywhere."

Deadalus thought for a moment and then shrugged.

"We'll just have to do without him, I guess."

They went into the mess room where the men were gathered. Deadalus looked over the faces. There was hardly a man who didn't have a wound of some kind.

"I have a little proposition for you," Deadalus began. "This starship we're in used to belong to the Empirical secret police. There is no better fighting machine. I propose that we use it to give back to the Empire some of what it's been giving everyone else."

There was a boisterous cheer from the men that belied their feeble appearance.

Deadalus held up his hand for attention.

"Wait, before you decide, let me explain. There is absolutely no way that we can beat the

Empire. They have too many men and too many ships for us to delude ourselves into believing that we have any chance whatsoever of beating them."

A silence met his words.

"If we declare war on the Empire, it will only be a matter of time before they catch us, and when they catch us, they won't take prisoners. It may be a matter of days, months, or even years depending on how good we are, but in the end they will get us. We're not going to beat them, but we will win. Everyday that we manage to stay alive, we'll have won. Every time we inflict more harm on them than they do on us, we'll have won. We won't beat them, but we will win, just as we won today."

The crowd shouted their agreement.

Whiskey came in the mess room, his jaw set defiantly. He walked to the front of the group. Deadalus looked at him and saw that the young man was thinking of Flo.

"Where have you been, Whiskey?" Deadalus asked.

"I've been out for a walk."

There was complete silence in the room as everyone turned their attention to Whiskey.

"You see, Captain, I figured that this motley crew was going to need a name of some kind. So I took the liberty of painting a new name on the starship."

Whiskey turned and faced the rest of the men.

"Most of you men were born and raised on Eurydice, like I was. You've lived there your whole life. But now she's gone, you can never have her back. So I chose a name to help us remember what we've lost. With your permission Captain, I've named the starship—Orpheus."

There was a silence as the words sunk in, and then loud agreement from the men. Whiskey turned and met Deadalus's eye.

"Just so we don't forget what it is we're fighting for," the younger man said.

Deadalus nodded slowly. He was going to remember what he had lost. And he wasn't going to let anyone else forget it either.

Especially Chief Hissler.

RICHARD BLADE

by Jeffrey Lord

More bestselling heroic fantasy from Pinnacle, America's #1 series publisher.
Over 3.5 million copies of Blade in print!

CELEBRATING 10 YEARS IN PRINT
AND OVER 22 MILLION COPIES SOLD!